"Stop living in the past!"

Craig sounded curiously angry. "Ned's dead, Jeanette. Accept it. But don't bury your heart with him. You can't stay single for the rest of your life."

"Why can't I?" Jeanette countered lightly, disguising the underlying tremor in her voice. "I can never marry—not now. But I can't tell you why." She turned away to hide the tears in her eyes.

"You don't have to explain," he said. "I know why. You're in love with a man you can't possibly have."

Jeanette smiled bitterly. Craig was right. She did want a man who was beyond her reach, but it wasn't Ned. It was Craig himself.

Beyond the Sweet Waters

by

ANNE HAMPSON

Harlequin Books

TORONTO • LONDON • LOS ANGELES • AMSTERDAM
SYDNEY • HAMBURG • PARIS • STOCKHOLM • ATHENS • TOKYO

Original hardcover edition published in 1970
by Mills & Boon Limited

ISBN 0-373-01467-8

Harlequin edition published February 1971
Second printing February 1977
Third printing January 1979
Fourth printing May 1979
Fifth printing August 1979
Sixth printing December 1979
Seventh printing April 1980
Eighth printing January 1981
Ninth printing July 1981

Printed in Canada

CHAPTER ONE

JEANETTE stood by the open window of her room gazing across the strait to the shadowed slopes of the Asian shore.

The familiar scene unfolded as the burning glow of the sunset spread like molten lava over the calm waters of the Bosphorus. Twinkling lights began to appear from the fishermen's lanterns, and from the tiny villages along the waterfront.

Voices from below brought a momentary frown to her brow as tranquillity gave place to a strange feeling of unrest. Craig Fleming had come to dine with them; he and her brother, Mark, were talking in the garden.

A month had passed since her first meeting with Craig. He had called on the day of her arrival. His stay was short, his greeting cool, and Jeanette had soon realized that the visit was made merely as an act of courtesy to his friend, and not owing to any desire to meet Jeanette herself. His grandmother had belonged to the old aristocracy that had been settled in Istanbul for many generations; from her he had inherited an air of almost majestic superiority which, to Jeanette, contrasted disconcertingly with her own lack of confidence.

Turning to the mirror, she picked up a comb, holding it for a moment as she contemplated her reflection.

Warned by Mark that she would receive invitations to dinners, dances and various Consulate functions, she had spent a good deal of her savings on her wardrobe. The blue cocktail dress embossed with gold and silver thread was one of her most expensive purchases, but she knew it suited her, accentuated the slender lines of her body. It matched her eyes which, wide and pensive, stared back at her with a brooding expression. Slowly she drew the comb through her hair; it fell, straight and fair, on to her shoulders.

As usual, she was delaying the meeting with Craig, and with a resolute, almost impatient gesture, she replaced the comb and made her way downstairs and out to the garden.

Coloured lanterns in the trees provided a soft and subtle illumination. Tony, who shared the house with Mark, had joined the others, and they were all sitting at a small wicker table where Mark was pouring drinks.

Jeanette stood for a moment in the shadows, scarcely aware of the interchange of conversation, or the chug chug of the motor boats in the distance, for her whole attention was on Craig. He was leaning back in his chair, and there was a suggestion of arrogance even in the movements of his fingers idly tapping the arm. His face was half turned towards her, a handsome face but proud ... too proud. The dark hair and fine arch of the brows, the firm set of the jaw ... all contributed to that impression of power and strength which had disturbed her from the moment they had met.

That his presence could make the past seem dim and unreal filled her with unreasoning resentment towards him. At home her thoughts had remained loyal to Ned – Ned, who loved swimming, and who had been caught unawares.

The old pain returned as she recalled the happy days of their brief engagement. At twenty-two she had been in her first year at the grammar school where she taught history; Ned had just been made a partner in the firm for which he worked.

How rosy their future – and how quickly it had all changed.

For a long while Jeanette could see nothing to live for. The future now appeared as an endless void. Three years had passed, and though the wound had healed the scar remained. Although aware of her mother's anxiety, and that she hoped someone would eventually take Ned's place, Jeanette had shunned men's company, and the long, self-inflicted solitude had made her shy and awkward when in their presence.

Then Mark had gone over to Istanbul for a year as guest lecturer on nuclear physics at the university. Two months later he wrote suggesting she come out to him; there was a vacancy at the school in Beyoğlu and he could obtain it for her. A complete change of surroundings was just what she needed, her mother had said, and Jeanette had agreed to go merely to please her and to relieve her anxiety.

On arrival she had been enchanted with her new home, for it was one of the ultra-modern villas in Ortaköy, the delightful suburb on the shores of the Bosphorus. Only the wealthy could afford to live in Ortaköy – the old aristocracy, business men, and men like Craig, who was manager for a world-famous oil company. Mark, and his friend Tony Powell, also a lecturer at the university, had been fortunate in renting the house from a family who were touring Europe for a year.

Jeanette felt she would never forget her first glimpse of the house. Standing in extensive grounds which ran right down to the shores of the Bosphorus, it had superb views over the strait. Judas trees and lilacs blossomed among the palms, and the air was filled with the scent of jasmine. Behind Ortaköy the hills, covered with jacarandas, had appeared to be draped in a soft blue mist.

With the house had gone Metat, gardener and odd-job man, who also waited on them at table. He was small and old, with the forlorn, hang-dog demeanour so characteristic of the poorer classes of Turks. The housekeeper, too, had also to be taken over, although she spoke only Turkish, much to the dismay of her new employers.

Realizing that Craig had turned his head, as if aware of her presence, Jeanette moved forward and sat down. 'Vodka?' asked Mark, but she shook her head. He and Tony glanced at her with their usual appreciation; to her surprise, Craig's eyes also flickered with interest. His voice, however, still held the familiar coolness as he bade her 'Good evening'.

Almost immediately Metat appeared to say that the dinner would be delayed for about half an hour. Jeanette rose again. Tony and Mark were discussing their work; Craig had returned to his perusal of *The Yachtsman* which lay open on his knee.

'I think I'll go for a walk,' she said. 'You don't mind?' The three were included in her glance and Mark and Tony shook their heads.

'You'll need a wrap,' Mark said.

'Oh, I'm quite warm.' The climate was still a novelty. She delighted in being able to go about without a coat.

'You will need one,' her brother insisted. 'The breeze coming over the Bos can be quite cool on occasions.'

'But I'm sure I won't be cold—'

'Let Metat fetch it for you.' Craig's deep voice cut her short. Was he really concerned for her welfare? – or merely irritated by her argument? Whatever the reason for his interference she was taken aback by it, and she stared at him wonderingly for a moment. Then, with a wry smile, she said it would be quicker to fetch the wrap herself than try and explain what she wanted to Metat. Craig then spoke to him in Turkish and within a few minutes the old man returned with the wrap, which he handed to Craig. After a slight hesitation he stood up and put it round Jeanette's shoulders. Again she stared. For a month he had scarcely noticed her, at times had almost ignored her presence. But tonight he seemed so different, so ... human, and she was reminded of what Mark had said soon after her arrival.

'His hobby is archaeology; with your own interest in it, and your knowledge of history, you should get on well together.'

They had certainly not got on well together up till now. Not that it mattered, Jeanette told herself, though she did wonder why there was such constraint between them. With Mark's other friends she had managed to adopt the friendly, free-and-easy manner which had come so naturally in the days before her long period of

8

seclusion. It was impossible to remain shy and awkward when Mark and Tony had so many friends coming to the house. She no longer felt shy with Craig, but they seemed to have so little in common that conversation between them was always difficult and strained.

He surprised her even further by saying,

'I feel like a walk myself. I'll come along with you — if you don't mind.'

She frowned. She did mind, though she could scarcely say so. She loved walking alone; it gave her a sense of peace and contentment.

They proceeded in silence for some moments, then Jeanette stopped.

'I hope I shall never come to take this for granted.' Her eyes eagerly took in the enchanting scene of a myriad twinkling lights reflected in the calm waters of the strait. Countless small fishing boats bobbed about in leisurely fashion. Each had two men, one holding the lantern while the other dragged the net. A clear, crescent moon was reflected in the water, and the ripples shone like silver. Along the gently-curving waterfront the picturesque old *yalis* lent an air of mystery and stimulated the imagination. These wooden houses had an abundance of ornate carving laced in intricate patterns; the lower windows were covered with delicate tracery which had enabled the Turkish ladies to see out without being observed themselves. What were they like inside? wondered Jeanette. She could ask Craig, for he owned one on Büyük Ada, one of the Princes' islands in the Sea of Marmara. But he might consider it tantamount to asking for an invitation, especially as Mark had stayed there on several occasions, so she remained silent, preferring to ask her brother about it later.

'Has the Bosphorus cast its spell over you, too?' Craig asked with a smile.

'Yes . . . do you feel like this?'

'I'm used to it, of course, but much of its charm persists.'

'Have you lived here a long time? I know you were educated in England, but – you were born here?'

'I was born here, yes, but we left soon afterwards. My parents had too many ties in our own country and couldn't settle here. But we often came over to see my grandmother.'

'And now you have returned for good?'

'Not for good. I'm here merely because the firm sent me. I was in Greece until four years ago and eventually I shall settle there, probably in a couple of years or so.'

In two years' time he hoped to settle in Greece. . . . Did he hope that Diane would be free by then? – free to come over here and marry him? For some reason she could not define she had no wish to think of Diane, the woman so precious to him that he had spent his youth in waiting, and longing. . . .

At times Jeanette could not imagine his loving any woman; at others she could believe he'd have one woman in his life, and one only – and that was exactly what he had done.

Jeanette felt an inexplicable tightness in her throat as they walked on again. In spite of herself she could not keep her thoughts from straying to Diane, whom she had never seen, but whom she could visualize so clearly from her brother's description.

Craig and Mark had been at university together, but had lost touch for over ten years until meeting again by accident in Istanbul. Diane, also a student at the university, had, according to Mark, 'been blessed by the gods in both looks and disposition'. All the male students, including Mark, had had a crush on her, but she had eyes only for Craig. Both were just nineteen at the time.

Then tragedy had come to Diane. Her mother, widowed when quite young, had remarried, and when she and her husband died within a few months of each other their four young children were in danger of becoming separated.

Roy Denton, son of a wealthy business man, had always admired Diane, and he offered to care for the children and bring them up as his own if she would marry him. Craig and Diane talked this over and agreed to part for the sake of the children. Soon after the marriage Diane learned that Roy had a rare and incurable bone disease, but would probably live for several years. On discovering this Craig vowed to wait for Diane, Mark had stated, though adding, 'or so it's believed'.

'You appear to be more settled at school.' Craig's voice broke into her musings, and she felt oddly grateful to him for the diversion. 'Mark mentioned you were having some difficulty.'

'Yes, but I'm enjoying it now that I've become used to the children.' The school catered for the children of business men and Consulate officials, and although Jeanette had only sixteen in her class, there were seven nationalities among them. 'The language problem rather frightened me at first, but most of the children speak some English, so I'm beginning to manage very well.'

'I thought you would soon find a way of solving the problem,' and, before she could take that as praise, 'English teachers would obviously not be employed unless such difficulties could be overcome.' He paused. 'And the staff – are you quite happy with them?'

'Quite. I've made two friends – English girls. They have a flat near the shore at Tophane. They've been showing me round some of the night clubs and restaurants.'

'From what I can gather you've been having a rather hectic night life since you came over here.' Craig's tones were dry.

'Yes, indeed. Mark and Tony have taken me about a good deal, too.' She hesitated. 'I want to get round to the really important places, though. I haven't done much sightseeing yet.'

'Surely you've done all the usual round?' His brows lifted in surprise as she shook her head.

'I've visited several mosques, and St. Sophia, but I haven't had much time. With finding things so difficult at school I've spent every week-end preparing lessons. I'm fairly well organized now so I shall have more time. I did hope to visit the Palace on Saturday, but Mark and Tony are both attending some function at the university, so neither is free to go with me.'

'What about your two friends? Can't they go with you?'

'Not this week-end; they've been invited out.'

Craig paused, as if in careful deliberation.

'In that case,' he said at last, 'I shall have to take you myself.'

An astounded silence followed. He couldn't possibly wish to take her on a sightseeing tour. He had obviously felt obliged to make the offer, and Jeanette rebelled at the idea of his escorting her for that reason.

'Thank you, but I'm sure you would find it boring. You must have visited all of the places many times.' The slight tartness in her voice instantly found response in his.

'Had I expected to be bored I shouldn't have made the suggestion! I'll pick you up on Saturday just after lunch – or do you wish to go before?'

Again her anger rose as his tone implied that he expected no further opposition. Typical of him to assume she would readily fall in with his plan. In the short time she had known him she had discovered that, when he made a decision, he expected everyone concerned to accept it – which they invariably did. Much to her annoyance Jeanette found herself doing the same.

'It's up to you; I really don't mind.' And then, 'Perhaps a whole day would be too much?'

'You would certainly find it tiring. In any case, even a whole day at Topkapi wouldn't suffice. You'll need to visit it many times in order to appreciate its numerous treasures.'

Now that the arrangements were actually made Jeanette forgot her annoyance and found herself looking forward eagerly to the visit. She certainly could have no better guide than Craig, who was so familiar with the ancient city and its world-famous buildings.

They had been strolling in the direction of Craig's own house, and she could just discern the graceful lines of his yacht straining gently at its moorings. At the same time she became aware of a large motor launch skimming smoothly towards them over the rising waves. The launch was heading south, and as Jeanette speculated on its destination she remembered that Craig had spent every week-end for the past month at his house on Büyük Ada. In his spare time he was writing a book on the site at Santorini, where he had spent a year on excavations before coming to Istanbul, and for this he preferred the peaceful atmosphere of his island retreat where he would not be disturbed by visitors.

'What about your book? Aren't you going to your island?'

'*My* island?' He sounded amused, but added, more seriously, 'I can leave it for one week-end; the rest won't do me any harm.' He paused and she felt he was frowning. 'As a matter of fact, it's not coming along as well as I would wish.'

She eyed him in some surprise. He gave so strong an impression of efficiency, of the ability to overcome all obstacles, that the admission seemed totally out of character.

'You mean – you can't concentrate?'

'That's about it.'

Yes, he was much more human tonight, and this encouraged her to suggest that he might be overworking. She knew his job was exacting and entailed a good deal of travelling to all parts of the country. It was not only concerned with the import and refining of the oil, but also with the numerous by-products. He was interested, too, in investigating the extent of the country's own reserves with a view to cutting down the quantity of imported oil.

'No, it isn't the job,' he replied after a long pause. 'It's ... well, one has to have a completely calm and untroubled mind in order to concentrate.'

Could it be the thought of Diane that disturbed the calmness of his mind? Was it impatience? Had the waiting, now that it must surely be nearing its end, become more irksome?

For no apparent reason the night had suddenly lost its charm.

'I'd like to go back,' she said, in a flat tone. The brief friendliness was gone; silence descended like a wall between them and both were profoundly conscious of the old restraint.

Craig left soon after dinner, and as Tony went to the study to prepare a lecture, Mark and Jeanette were left alone. Mark poured himself a drink, then sat down with the newspaper. Picking up a book, Jeanette tried to read, but could not fix her attention to it. She felt impatient with the confusion of her mind; so many visions were superimposed one upon another. Ned, whom no one could ever replace; Craig, whom she should have been able to dismiss from her mind without undue effort. And there was Diane. . . .

Why this desire to know more about her? Jeanette, puzzling over this, sighed impatiently.

Mark was engrossed in his reading, but she interrupted him, saying, with assumed carelessness,

'What was Diane like?' Her question must sound strange, she thought, but to her relief Mark showed no surprise as he looked up, his eyes oddly bright and eager.

'I told you, she was something special – every man's dream of the perfect girl. She must have been fully aware of herself because everyone loved her. The most amazing thing was that she remained completely unaffected by all the adulation which was bestowed upon her. She and Craig made a handsome pair; wherever they went people turned to look at them.' His thoughts seemed far away and Jeanette found herself saying gravely, and with some concern,

14

'Were you hurt? – when she chose Craig?'

'Oh, no. We all knew there was no hope for any of us.' He spoke quickly, carelessly. 'You know how it is, though, when you're young; you get these crushes. But we were all too wise to fall heavily.' Again his thoughts seemed distant, and Jeanette watched him in silence for a while.

He had the same build as Craig, and the same dark hair, but there was about him an attractive gentleness lacking in Craig. The lines of his face, too, were softer and he smiled more often. He was extraordinarily good-looking, she thought, with a little access of pride. He glanced up, as if expecting her to continue the conversation.

'Have they met since? I mean, recently?'

'At first they made a clean break, which was of course the only sensible thing to do; they didn't know of Roy's illness at the time. But from what Craig has said it would appear that they did meet fairly regularly before he left England. I don't suppose they actually went out to-gether – Craig would not have done anything to hurt Roy – but they probably met at his mother's home. Mrs. Fleming and Diane have always remained friends and they visit one another. It broke Mrs. Fleming's heart when they parted, and I'm sure she still thinks there's no other woman good enough for her son.'

'And you? Have you seen her?' Jeanette immediately wondered what had prompted the question, for it seemed quite irrelevant.

'I saw her last year—' Mark broke off abruptly and sat musing for a while. 'She'd been shopping and was having lunch at a small café where I usually took mine. It was a pleasant surprise for us both, and of course we talked a lot about the old days. She looked as attractive as ever, though older, but you would never have taken her for thirty-four. Considering the trouble she's had with Roy, and the responsibility of bringing up those kids, she looked remarkably youthful. There are no money worries, and I suppose that helps.' He paused, and Jeanette noticed the admiration in his eyes, and wondered at it.

'She asked me to go back with her and have a chat with Roy. He was in a wheelchair, poor devil, but as happy and cheerful as you please. He adores Diane, and whatever she feels for him, she has given him some very happy years.' There was another pause before he went on, 'They appear to be suited and content – Roy obviously is, but Diane . . . well, I sometimes wonder.'

'She could have come to love him,' suggested Jeanette, and her brother smiled.

'I don't profess to know much about women,' he said wryly, 'but I imagine it would be difficult to love anyone else after Craig.' Jeanette glanced sharply at him, struck by an odd note in his voice, and he continued quickly, 'There's respect, no doubt about that. It couldn't be otherwise, the way he suffers without complaining. And Diane must be exceedingly grateful to him, for he's given those children everything. I told you how well they had all done?'

She nodded. One of the boys was a doctor and the other a partner in a firm of lawyers. The two girls had their own beauty salon, bought for them by Roy.

'The children must be very grateful, too,' murmured Jeanette, thinking that Roy must be a truly wonderful person, and wondering why such people had to suffer.

'They are, and I'm glad to say they show their gratitude.' He went on to say that Diane's task was now completed and, as Roy's illness was progressing more rapidly, it could not be long before Diane was free to find happiness. 'I think I mentioned that Craig had said Roy was much worse when his mother last wrote?'

'Yes. . . . And then Diane will come out here and marry Craig, do you think?' Jeanette's voice was not quite steady, and a dryness caught her throat.

'I suppose so.' Mark's tones were sharp and his brow creased in a frown. 'At least, that's what everyone expects will happen, and yet. . . .'

'Yes?' Why did she sound so breathless? And why should she wait so expectantly for her brother's reply?

'Well, fifteen years is a long time; people change.'

'But if they were really in love?'

'They were.' Mark was emphatic about that. 'Only—' He shrugged. 'I suppose they'll do what pleases them.' Rising, he poured himself another drink. Clearly he no longer wished to continue the conversation.

Jeanette's friends, Sally and Gwen, were decorating. They had moved into the flat at Tophane only six weeks previously, after having lived for eight months under the most primitive conditions in the Fatih district where the old wooden houses were literally falling to pieces around them. This accommodation had been found for them on their taking up their appointments. Soon they began looking round for a more suitable flat, but rents were so exorbitant that the search had taken longer than anticipated. Eventually they had found the charming flat at Tophane, and had moved in, although the rent was out of all proportion to their salaries.

Having offered to help, Jeanette arrived at the flat early in the evening. Gwen was up the ladder, Sally pasting at the table. Both were being watched by an audience of Turkish gentlemen consisting of Ali, the caretaker of the flats, Selim, his son, and Ismet, the wizened old man who kept the grocery store along the street.

Staring in puzzlement from Gwen to the three fascinated onlookers, and then to Sally, Jeanette inquired if anything was wrong.

Gwen, flushed and dishevelled, and swearing softly but genteelly as a corner of the paper came away on her duster, twisted round on her precarious perch.

'You may well ask!' Her dark eyes laughed with sheer amusement, contrasting with the hint of impatience in her voice. 'Believe it or not, none of these has ever set eyes on a roll of wallpaper before. We never thought when we let Ali in to fix the latch on the balcony window – he almost collapsed when he saw us actually fixing paper to the walls. Then he disappeared, and we assumed he'd taken fright and made a quick getaway from these mad English, but we should have known better. Back he comes rushing, with these two, and we just can't get rid of them.'

'They haven't ever seen wallpaper?' gasped Jeanette. 'They must have!'

'Ask them then,' suggested Gwen impishly and Jeanette had to laugh. As she spoke no Turkish and they no English, communication was impossible. She had the greatest admiration for Gwen who, completely undaunted, somehow managed to get through to these people by a mixture of pidgin Turkish, intelligent guesswork and the most expressive miming. Inevitably there were occasions when this misfired, resulting in what Gwen, with her incredible good humour and calm, laughingly described as 'rather disturbing misadventures'. There was, for example, the time when Gwen had instructed Mrs. 'Sparrow', who cleaned for them, to give everything an extra polish, as she and Sally were giving a party. That conscientious lady, with painstaking thoroughness, had turned the hosepipe on the walls – without even the forethought to remove the carpet beforehand!

'If they don't have wallpaper here, then where did you get it?' Jeanette wanted to know.

'From home – brought it back with us after the Christmas holidays,' Sally put in. 'Good thing no one decided to examine the contents of the car. You never know how these people are going to react. Might have thought it was some sort of secret weapon we'd brought over to blow up the Galata Bridge or something.'

This brought a peal of laughter from Gwen and Jeanette, and they were joined by the three men. Donning her overall, Jeanette began clearing up the scraps of paper adhering to the floor.

'Can't we just shoo them off?' suggested Sally after a while. 'I never work well when I'm being watched.' She paused, eyeing the men up and down. 'Wouldn't be so bad if they were young and handsome, but a more unprepossessing bunch I've yet to meet!'

The men apparently thought they were being flattered. They gave Sally a broad grin before settling themselves against the wall as if preparing for a long stay. Always the men here seemed to be leaning against something, idling away their time, Jeanette had noticed.

She took over the pasting and soon they were working expertly as a team. After a short while Mrs. Sparrow appeared. Small and spare, she wore a black dress buttoned right up to the neck, and on her arms were about a dozen bangles, all gold. This was the way the poorer, working class women saved their money.

After many vain attempts to pronounce her name, the girls had christened her Mrs. Sparrow, and the reason for this was easy to see. Chirpy as a bird, always in a hurry, she flitted about all over the place. Her small head bobbed this way and that and, to complete the impression, she had a rather long, pointed nose. She jabbered away to Gwen, who was trying to concentrate on what she said while at the same time endeavouring to match the pattern on a wall which was about six inches out of true.

'What is it all about?' asked Jeanette, puzzled. 'I thought Mrs. Sparrow didn't come in the evenings.'

'Afraid of missing something,' replied Sally. 'Gwen told her earlier that we were going to decorate.'

'She has just expressed the opinion that we're quite mad,' interposed Gwen calmly. 'She finds it inconceivable that anyone in her right mind would put paper on a wall.'

It was Mrs. Sparrow, however, who rid them of their audience. Being less tolerant than the girl, she hustled the men to the door within minutes of her arrival and they made their way reluctantly downstairs.

'The milk!' Gwen almost toppled off the ladder. Jeanette stepped aside in alarm as she sped like a whirlwind to the top of the stairs. 'Too late.' Gwen returned and went over to the balcony rail, where she stood uttering the most blood-curdling shrieks, while Jeanette listened in astounded silence. Although she had been friendly with the girls for nearly five weeks, she still did not know what to expect next.

'Just ordering the milk from Ismet,' Sally obliged, sensing her bewilderment. 'All that is Gwen's own particular brand of Turkish for, "as much as you can spare tomorrow, please". You see, Turkish cows go dry for about three days a week, so we have to stock up.' She was on her knees, measuring off a length of paper from the roll which was spread out along the floor. Her eyes were alight with laughter as she looked up to meet Jeanette's sceptical gaze. 'Honest – at least, that's the conclusion we've come to, because there are days when it's quite impossible to buy milk anywhere.'

When at last the final length of paper was fixed, the three girls stood in the middle of the room admiring the results of their work. Mrs. Sparrow, wagging her head from side to side, indicated her approval, after which she made them coffee and sandwiches and then went home. They took their supper out on to the balcony. It was early June; the night air, soft as silk, was stirred gently by a faint breeze coming up from the south. The flat had a magnificent view over the outer harbour of the Golden Horn to Seraglio Point and the Sea of Marmara beyond. Numerous small motor-craft and *kayiks* fishing by the Galata Bridge sent out their flickering lights to mingle with those along the Golden Horn. Cupolas of the mosques stood out sharply in the lights of the city and the slender minarets were silhouetted against an amethyst sky. Gwen leant back in her chair with a contented sigh.

'I'm glad we decided to take it,' she said. 'Always fancied myself in a place with a balcony overlooking the sea. Makes me feel like a millionaire.'

'Talking of millionaires,' put in Sally, turning to Jeanette, 'how is your friend, Craig Fleming?'

Jeanette gave a rather startled little laugh.

'Shouldn't think he's a millionaire – he seems to work extremely hard for his money.' And he is not my friend, she added, though silently.

'Well, those oil managers always seem like million-aires, with their great flashy cars and chauffeurs and yachts.'

'He writes books.' Sally helped herself to another sandwich. 'We read his last one because it was about an archaeological site in Western Turkey which Gwen and I had visited. Craig Fleming was lucky to get permission to dig there, for the Turks are not like the Greeks. They have even better sites than those of Greece, but seem deter-mined not to have them excavated.'

Jeanette had also read the book and they discussed its merits for a while and then she decided it was time she went home. Tony had brought her, for he was visiting friends in the old part of the city, but as he was uncertain as to the time of his return, it was arranged that Gwen should run Jeanette home.

Just as they were preparing to go they heard a call from below, and Gwen invited their visitor to come up.

'Çetin,'she said, and they all sat down again. They were not surprised at the lateness of the visit, for it was quite customary for people to drop in on their friends after visiting a night club or restaurant. Jeanette was used to it by now, for Mark's friends also came and went at the oddest hours.

Çetin Rustem was just one of a cosmopolitan crowd of young people with whom the two girls had become friendly since their arrival in Istanbul ten months ago. Jeanette had first met him at the Italian Consulate, when attending a dinner dance there with Sally and Gwen. She had met him several times since, for he was a frequent visitor to the flat. He was an officer at the Naval Train-ing College, and as Jeanette turned to smile a welcome she thought how handsome he looked in his white uniform which contrasted so strongly with his deep tan and raven hair. Declining Gwen's offer of supper, he said he was just passing and decided to drop in for a few minutes only. His English was excellent, as was that of many other officers of the college, and he had a charm of manner that even Jeanette found most attractive.

He was an expert climber and had been trying for months to persuade the two girls to join one of his parties; he looked keenly disappointed as they now refused another invitation.

'We will come one of these week-ends,' Sally promised, and with that he had to be satisfied. They all chatted for a short while and then, as Çetin was going the same way as Jeanette, he offered to see her home.

He dropped her at the front door, but instead of entering the house she stood for a moment enjoying the deep silence. The night was clear and warm, with millions of stars above and the calm sea gleaming below. On sudden impulse she went out through the garden again, feeling exhilarated as she walked briskly in the direction of Craig's house. She had gone only a short distance when her heart gave a lurch as she sensed she was no longer alone. Turning, she saw a man coming quickly towards her and, although she was not of a nervous disposition, her first impulse was to run. But which way? If she turned back she could not reach her gate before he did, yet there seemed no point in going forward. How stupid to decide on taking a walk at this hour! Making an effort to quell her fears she continued to walk on, but in spite of herself her heart began to race painfully and her legs felt weak. The entrance to Craig's garden offered safety and she hastened towards it, hoping desperately that she would reach it before the man caught up with her. At last, breathless, she entered the path and walked a short distance before stopping in the shadow of the hedge. She must have gained on the man, for he did not appear for a while. Then he passed without even a glance in the direction she had taken; at the same time she heard Craig's voice, deeply concerned.

'Jeanette, what on earth is wrong? Has something happened to Mark?'

'No ... no, it isn't anything serious.' Jeanette flushed with embarrassment, realizing how foolish her explanation would sound. 'I thought I'd take a walk – then I saw a man behind me and I took fright and came in here.'

There was a moment's astounded silence during which all his concern vanished.

'Do you mean to say you had no more sense than to walk along the shore at this hour!' His tone was sharp to the point of anger, but in her relief she took no exception to it.

'I realize it was silly – but it's such a lovely night.'

'Silly? It was the height of madness. Don't ever do such a thing again!' He still seemed unable to understand so foolish an action, and added, 'What made you decide to come out here at two in the morning? Can't you sleep?'

'I was already out.' She went on to explain what had happened, but immediately she mentioned Çetin she regretted it, for she knew that Craig disliked him intensely.

'Çetin!' His tones were even sharper than before. 'This is no time of the morning to be out with a man like Çetin!'

The implication brought spots of angry colour to her cheeks, but she managed to control her voice.

'He merely gave me a lift home. As he was coming this way, it seemed the sensible thing to do. It saved Gwen coming out.'

Ignoring that, Craig said he would walk back with her and they went down the path to the shore. Jeanette felt grateful for his company, guilty at having brought him out, and miserable because she had made such a fool of herself.

The sitting-room light was on when they reached the house, and they could see Metat tidying up, but there was no sign of Mark or Tony.

'They appear to be in bed.' Craig beckoned to Metat to open the window for Jeanette to enter. She thanked him for bringing her home, hoping the slight tremor of dejection would escape his notice. When he spoke again it was in a much softer tone, though with the same stern inflection.

'You'll be well advised to keep Rustem at a distance, and on no account must you join one of his climbing parties.' His last words were actually an order, which Jeanette resented, but again she remained calm. Friction between them must be avoided, not only because he was Mark's good friend, but also because tomorrow was Saturday, and they could hardly set out on a sightseeing trip in an atmosphere of unfriendliness. However, she hoped her silence would not lead him into the mistaken belief that she intended obeying his order. In fact, she made the firm resolve that, should Çetin wish to include her in one of his climbing parties, she would accept without hesitation.

CHAPTER TWO

To Jeanette's surprise Murad, the chauffeur, was driving when Craig called for her the following afternoon. Owing to the large number of thieves in the city he preferred not to leave the car unattended, Craig explained as he took his place beside her in the back seat.

Their way ran along the coast, past the Çeregan and Dolmabahçe Palaces in a southerly direction towards the Galata Bridge. On the bridge itself the usual chaos prevailed. There was congestion and confusion everywhere as the teeming mass of vehicles and pedestrians surged in both directions. The car crawled, the delay being caused by a cart drawn by oxen. No one appeared to mind, no one was in a hurry.

Although she had fitted into the life as naturally as if she had lived there some considerable time, Jeanette was still fascinated by the city, that meeting place of east and west with its three thousand years of history. Ancient capital of the Ottoman Empire, it had the mysterious, fairy-tale-like quality of the Orient in spite of the fact that it was rapidly becoming westernized. Strange contrasts were everywhere apparent. American luxury cars moved alongside little grey donkeys, their backs laden with fruit and vegetables; modern German buses were held up by horse-drawn carts. The architecture, too, presented the same diversity. The old wooden houses, and modern blocks of buildings; the Ottoman mosques and Byzantine churches. There were the wealthy ladies with their hired *hamals*, carrying their parcels; there were the black-capped, moustached Anatolian peasants, hollow-cheeked and careworn, scouring the city in search of work, their wives trudging wearily a few paces behind.

'What an antiquated custom!' Jeanette frowned her disgust. 'Why does it persist, I wonder?'

'Quite a good idea.' Craig followed the direction of her gaze. 'Keeps the woman in her place.'

Jeanette's eyes flashed as she turned to look up at him. His glance was half amused, half mocking. Impossible to tell whether or not the remark was to be taken seriously. It certainly did not reflect his opinion of all women, she decided, thinking for a moment of Diane.

The old Seraglio, or Topkapi-Saray, as the Palace was called by the Turks, had no systematic plan, for successive Sultans had made their own additions throughout the years. It followed the idea of the ancient Byzantine imperial palaces in that it consisted of kiosks, mosques, fountains, gateways and numerous other ornate buildings dotted about the gardens amid cypresses and plane trees.

'Take your sun-glasses,' Gwen had warned. 'Topkapi just drips with diamonds and rubies and gold and silver!'

That, Jeanette soon decided, was in fact an understatement. Never had she dreamed that so much wealth could have been brought together in one collection. Moving from one massive hall full of treasure to another, she became almost speechless with wonder. In one room alone, Craig told her, the gems were estimated to be worth ten million pounds. The throne, encrusted with thousands of emeralds, rubies and pearls, had been taken as spoil from the Shah of Persia's fabulous treasury. The royal cradle glittered with its fantastic ornamentation of precious stones.

'For the heir, I suppose.' Jeanette became lost in thought as she reflected on the fate of the Sultan's numerous younger sons. On his death they were strangled with a silken cord by order of their brother, the new Sultan. Some were only babies, but others were older, and she wondered how they could have resigned themselves to such a terrible fate. She mentioned this to Craig, who merely shrugged his shoulders before saying, without much interest,

'It was traditional. They were brought up to accept the inevitable.'

Frowning at this, Jeanette considered it for a while.

'They could have tried to escape,' she commented at length. 'I think they were stupid to accept it.'

'One must have somewhere to escape to,' replied Craig on an odd note. 'Quite often there isn't anywhere, in which case the sensible course is to resign oneself and accept what . . . life has to offer.' He turned to look at her squarely, and she knew he was not referring to the fate of the young princes.

'I – don't understand you,' she murmured, finding herself unable to hold his gaze.

'No? Then let me put it this way; those young men accepted death, but they also accepted life – took everything it had to give. There are some people, Jeanette, who persist in trying to escape from life.'

The precise meaning of his words still eluded her, though she had the sure conviction that it held both censure and warning. He could not mean that she was trying to escape from life . . . and yet. . . . Her brow creased in doubt. Was she accepting all that life had to offer? True, for three years she had lived almost as a recluse, her only interest being the lectures she had attended on archaeology at the university, but all that was now changed. She had friends, and belonged to the young and happy crowd that frequented the flat at Tophane. Her life was normal except for her attitude towards marriage. As she owed all her loyalty to Ned's memory, she could never marry, but Craig did not refer to that because he knew nothing about it – or did he? For the first time Jeanette fell to wondering just how much her brother had revealed about her.

'I still don't understand you,' she said at last, aware that he waited inquiringly for some comment.

'Don't you?' His tone was clipped and impatient. 'Very well, let's forget it.' And he moved to examine with apparent interest a collection of belts and clasps from the royal robes. Picking out certain items, he told her about the history, and the values, his eyes remaining cold even though Jeanette's widened in almost childish wonderment.

'A hundred thousand pounds for one clasp!' It was formed of three emeralds with a gold setting. 'Where did it all come from?'

'Gifts from monarchs to the reigning Sultan, mainly. It was collected over a period of five hundred years, remember.'

'Yes, of course.' They passed into other rooms, where in the great showcases gold and silver plate lay sadly covered with the dust of ages. So vast was the treasure that it was obviously impossible to keep it all clean.

'The rooms of the harem aren't open to the public,' Craig said, and she found herself sighing with relief. She felt so dazzled that she could not take in much more, she told him apologetically.

'I know how you feel; you'll derive greater benefit from small doses. We must come again in a week or two.' Despite this reference to another outing his tone remained cool and distant. The easy manner which had existed between them during the last couple of hours was gone and Jeanette sighed for its loss.

'You might like to see the kitchens, and then we'll go and have some tea.'

The kitchens were staggering in their size. Jeanette could not understand why they were so vast, or why there were so many of them.

'Not only the Sultan, but his mother, the wives, the chief eunuch and numerous other officials had their own private kitchens,' Craig explained as Jeanette stared in disbelief at the giant-sized utensils.

The kitchens housed a collection of over three thousand pieces of Chinese porcelain. There was a great deal of Ming, which Jeanette did not find particularly attractive; and the dishes and bowls which had huge rubies and emeralds stuck into their sides she found positively ugly. After wandering round on her own for a while she returned to Craig, who was so absorbed in the contents of one showcase that he appeared to be oblivious of everything going on around him.

'Oh, how lovely!' she exclaimed, and he turned in some surprise.

'Do you know anything about Celadons?' he asked curiously, his surprise increasing as she nodded.

'I studied the Sung dynasty for a while, and also attended a course on the pottery of the period. Then I was lucky enough to be invited to view the private collection of one of the lecturers.'

'You were lucky indeed. Did he happen to have a private fortune, too, this lecturer? He certainly didn't buy Celadons out of his salary.'

'His father left him money, and he used it in that way. He bought most of his pieces in China, but would travel to any part of the world if he knew there was a Celadon for sale.'

They stood in silence for some time, intent only on the exquisite simplicity of the vessels and bowls of incredible shades of blues and greens. Some bore faint marks of decoration; others were unadorned, and all had survived for nearly a thousand years.

An intimacy crept into their relationship as they stood together side by side, an intimacy born of their common interest, a love of beauty and antiquity. It swept away all restraint and brought them close for the very first time. Jeanette felt a strange happiness envelop her; it became revealed in her eyes and her smile as she moved her glance for a moment to turn to Craig. His own smile formed in quick response and he took her arm when, reluctantly, they both moved away.

Passing out through the 'Gate of Peace', they stopped for Craig to read the inscription which was written in Arabic above. It expressed the basic creed of Mohammedanism.

'There is no God but Allah, and Mohammed is the Prophet of Allah.'

The gate was flanked by tall towers; the chambers on

the left were equipped with everything required for executions, Craig informed her. Here condemned high court officials were beheaded.

'Only the Sultan was allowed to enter through this gate,' he went on, and then, in some amusement, 'If you're a romantic you can probably imagine him, in his splendid robes and jewelled turban, riding his magnificent steed— Or perhaps you would not consider that romantic?' He ended on a quizzical note and she laughed. When she spoke, however, her tones were serious.

'No, not when I remember the despotism of the rule. Turkey did well to rid herself of the Sultans.' Recalling that it was only forty-seven years since the last Sultan was deposed, she went on to ask curiously, 'I wonder what happened to the ladies of the harem? Some of them must be still living.'

'Many were returned to their families; the others – some of whom are now over eighty – are being cared for by the State.'

After having tea they wandered round the city for a while, as though anxious to prolong an afternoon that had proved so pleasant. They looked at the shops, at the colourful boats warped to the Galata Bridge, and at the fishermen, just standing about, apparently in no hurry to sell the fish they had caught.

'They have so many different kinds,' observed Jeanette, watching two men unload their boat. 'I've never seen so many fish.'

Craig explained that there were so many different currents and temperatures that the variety of plankton varied enormously and, consequently, the fish varied greatly, too.

There were street vendors everywhere, and rows of boot-blacks with their gleaming brass equipment. Suddenly realizing that she was constantly stopping to stare, Jeanette glanced up rather anxiously to discover what effect this had on Craig. Was he amused, bored, or actually impatient? Impossible to tell, for his calm demeanour revealed nothing. This did encourage her, however, as they neared the Sultan Ahmet Mosque, to suggest they enter it for a few moments. He nodded at once, as though the idea had already occurred to him.

In keeping with the Mohammedan ritual, they removed their shoes and, placing them on the rack, stepped out of the bright sunlight into the cool and dim interior of the mosque. A Turkish gentleman approached them. Tall and cultured, with bronzed skin and a mystic smile, he asked if they required a guide. Craig declined, but thanked him. He continued to accompany them, however, as they moved slowly over the thick carpets towards the white marble *minber*, talking of famous people who had visited the mosque. He talked a good deal of Mecca, though he had not yet made the sacred pilgrimage himself. Then, with a slight bow, he left them for a group of tourists who were staring somewhat vacantly about as if not quite knowing what they should do.

Jeanette stared up at the great towering dome and felt very small. She and Craig stood watching the row of workmen who, having taken time off from their labours, stood barefooted, their heads bowed in prayer.

'The Koran says the faithful must pray five times a day,' Craig whispered. 'They always pray at this hour – just before sunset.'

He lapsed into silence again and Jeanette gazed around her, marvelling at the massive pillars, the beautifully coloured windows and the numerous gold inscriptions – sacred writings from the Koran.

Over everything there shone the mysterious radiance effected by the blue tiles which decorated the walls; and in the atmosphere was felt the ever-present mellowness of age. Jeanette gave herself up to that sense of peace which she had experienced on a previous visit. Craig's hand on her arm, as he pointed out the highly ornate *mihrab*, awoke her from the sublime apathy into which she had fallen. She became profoundly aware of his nearness, and of the strengthening of the intimacy which had come upon them before leaving Topkapi.

The sun was setting as they came out into the courtyard again, and the great granite pillars were bathed in a deep crimson glow which contrasted eerily with the backcloth of ancient plane trees and the dark outlines of buildings scattered about the grounds. Lights began to appear all over the old part of the city, and also in Galata and Tophane through which they passed on their way home.

'Tired?' A mingling of gentleness and concern entered Craig's tone, for Jeanette had become oddly silent.

'A happy tiredness,' she smiled. 'I do thank you, Craig, for a wonderful afternoon.' Her smile deepened as she turned in the car, and her eyes were wide and filled with a new expression of which she was unaware. 'I shall always remember it.'

'So shall I,' he returned, and then, 'We must have another trip out soon. There's so much for you to see. Next week-end is out because of the Queen's official birthday celebrations on Saturday, and I shall be going down to Büyük Ada on Sunday – what about the following week-end?'

'That will be lovely!' Her eagerness brought a faint smile to Craig's lips. 'Where shall we go then?' She thought again about his book, wondering at his willingness to neglect it, for he had told Mark that he hoped to finish it by the end of the year.

'We certainly have plenty to choose from. Have you been over to the Asiatic side yet?' and when she shook her head, 'You'll like it. There are no large hotels, just quaint little fishing villages and ruined palaces – and, of course, the lovely stretch of country between Büyük Gok Su and Kücük Gok Su. Those are two little rivers that flow into the Bosphorus. The region is best known to us as the "Sweet Waters of Asia". When my grandmother was young it was the favourite rendezvous of high Ottoman society. The Turkish ladies would sail up Büyük Gok Su in their gilded barges, and a most wonderful sight it was.'

'It sounds fascinating.'

'Much of its Orientalism is now lost, of course, but its natural beauty remains unchanged. I'm sure you'll be delighted with it.'

By this time they had reached the drive and Jeanette offered to get out at the end, but Craig insisted on taking her to the door.

'Metat is in, I suppose?' he asked as she entered the hall.

'Oh, yes, he will be.' Jeanette looked about her vaguely. 'Well, Mrs. Baydur will be; she never goes out.'

Not satisfied, Craig followed her into the sitting-room. There was no sign either of Mrs. Baydur or Metat.

'Will Mark be very late?' he began, then saw Metat pass the window on his way in from the garden. 'Metat is in, so you'll be all right—' He broke off and, crossing the room, took a small object from the shelf in the corner. 'What's this?'

'I meant to ask you about it. I picked it up in a little shop where Sally and Gwen buy small antiques. What do you think about it?' She waited anxiously, and as he remained silent, examining it critically, she added, 'I – didn't pay much for it.' Still Craig continued to examine it with the touch of an expert, and after a while Jeanette suggested it might be a perfume jar.

'Yes, a perfume jar, certainly.' There was another long silence. 'It's exquisite. This is a real find, Jeanette.'

'Oh, Craig, is it really something special? I couldn't be sure, but I thought it might be. It's European, don't you agree?' His verdict had given her back the confidence she had had when buying it, and which she had begun to lose during his long deliberation. 'It has certain characteristics—' She broke off as Craig shook his head.

'Definitely not European.'

'But the clay, and texture?'

'No.' His reply was emphatic. He turned the little jar over and over, handling it almost with reverence as his

33

fingers moved across the surface with a gentleness that amazed her. What a strange man! One day he could be so arrogant and inflexible; another pleasant and companionable – and now. . . . She had never before seen him as human as this! He spoke at last, very quietly, but with conviction.

'Egyptian; about two thousand years old.'

Her eyes sparkled; she accepted his verdict without question.

'Two thousand? As old as that?'

'A rare find, indeed. Where did you say you bought it?'

'At a little shop – I don't think I could find it myself. Gwen and Sally took me. We went through the Grand Bazaar into a cobbled alleyway, and there was this shop, tucked right behind, and all grimy and full of junk.'

'Junk!' he exclaimed, and they both laughed. 'You must go along and find some more of this – er – junk.'

'We're going on Tuesday after school, but I don't suppose I'll find anything like this again.'

'It's extremely doubtful,' he agreed, and then, with a surprising twinkle in his eye, 'But you never know what else you may find. You could pick up a Celadon.'

'That's a very remote possibility, too,' she laughed. 'I don't suppose I shall ever start collecting those.'

He gave a gesture of agreement.

'You'll have to find yourself a husband with a ready-made collection.' His eyes still held amusement and his voice was light. Clearly he was joking, yet she stiffened at the mention of marriage and found herself unable to reply.

A change entered the atmosphere, almost imperceptible at first, but intensely apparent when, having replaced the jar, Craig turned to face her. Gone was the warmth of manner and amused expression. The more familiar hardness touched his mouth and his eyes glinted, cold as steel. Jeanette stared unbelievingly. What could have caused this sudden change in him?

'I must go,' he said brusquely. 'Don't stay up too late,

you've had a tiring afternoon.' And with that piece of advice he was gone.

What a strange ending to the wonderful hours they had spent together. Jeanette suddenly thought of Diane, and wondered if she really knew Craig, if she knew what a moody, unpredictable man she was going to marry.

'Why should I worry about Craig's moods – or Diane's future?' she asked herself impatiently as she went upstairs to wash and change for dinner. Craig was going to a dinner party given by one of the managers of another oil firm, and Jeanette found herself wishing she had accepted Çetin's invitation to dance with him at the Hilton. He had asked her to ring him if she changed her mind, and for a moment she felt tempted to do so. Then it occurred to her that Craig would most probably be at the Hilton, for quite often the managers held their dinner parties there. Craig disliked Çetin; also, he had advised her to have an early night and would, of course, expect her to follow that advice.

She decided against going out. For some inexplicable reason she felt reluctant to do anything of which Craig would not approve.

The following morning she was woken by the sun streaming through her window. She bathed and dressed in very brief shorts and a sun-top, and after breakfast she and the two men went into the garden, where Metat had set out the deck chairs on the lawn. Even at this early hour the sun created a quivering heat-haze over the strait, with the promise of a scorching day.

'Did you enjoy yourself yesterday?' inquired Tony, casting her an admiring glance as she sat down opposite to him.

'Yes, it was marvellous.' Her face became animated. 'Craig is so knowledgeable.'

'He's familiar with the city – he should be; he's lived here over four years, and before that he was a frequent visitor – till the death of his grandmother, that is.' Tony

35

picked up his newspaper, but made no attempt to open it.

'You weren't disappointed with Topkapi, then? Some people consider the main building a dreary sort of place.'

'I agree that the actual building isn't attractive,' she returned. 'But the treasures inside. . . .'

'Leave you speechless, eh?' Tony smiled. 'I went to the Palace once with Craig. Couldn't get him away from some old pots in the kitchen. Sing, or Sang—'

'Sung,' interrupted Jeanette laughingly. 'And *pots*! You have no soul, Tony!'

'Well, you'd find that Craig has a soul. How long did he stand there?'

'Some time – we both did; Craig seems extraordinarily interested in Celadons.'

'Naturally.' Mark glanced up from his book. 'He has a very fine collection himself.'

'Craig—?' Jeanette's eyes widened. 'Craig collects Celadons?'

'His grandmother started him off many years ago. I believe he has them packed away at his home in England at present – Is anything wrong?' Clearly Mark was puzzled by her expression.

'No – no, of course not.'

'You'll have to find yourself a husband with a ready-made collection. . . .'

Craig had been joking, no doubt about that . . . but what an odd thing to say. It was some considerable time before she was able to dismiss his words completely from her mind.

They spent the entire afternoon out of doors, having their meals on the patio and sunbathing in between. The air was balmy, the sun hot; they all relaxed contentedly, agreeing that they were really cut out for a life of ease, and deploring work in any form whatsoever. After dinner a cool breeze came across the strait and they were forced to go indoors. Tony and Mark settled down to a game of chess; Jeanette made no attempt to read, for she knew she would not concentrate, and she just sat there reflecting on the pleasant week-end she had spent. There had come to her a profound sense of peace which she accepted without any desire to know why or how it had happened.

The following week was the most trying she had experienced since coming to Istanbul. One of the teachers was ill and her class had been divided between Jeanette and Gwen. In addition, Jeanette had a new child, an Italian boy who spoke no English. She tried various means of getting through to him and failed, with the result that he became bored and she had a serious behaviour problem on her hands. Then two other children were fretful and it soon became apparent that they were sickening for hepatitis, which was prevalent in the city.

Altogether it was one of those weeks when she felt the children had drained her both mentally and physically. By Thursday she was so fatigued that on entering the staff-room she just flopped into a chair, limp and devoid of energy.

'You look all in, Jeanette. Off colour?' Miss Vicars, the art mistress, looking thoroughly true to type with her long straight hair and thick horn-rimmed spectacles, glanced at Jeanette in some anxiety. 'I hope you're not going to have jaundice.'

'I'm just tired, that's all.' Jeanette leant further back in her chair, putting a shaky hand to her head. She felt it was too much trouble even to speak.

'This heat doesn't help,' Gwen put in. 'I feel exhausted myself.' She glanced up from her marking. 'And if things aren't bad enough I have the dismal prospect of facing two irate mothers in the morning – and I'll wager neither can speak English.'

'Why, what's happened?' Sally had made the coffee and she brought over the tray and set it on a table in the centre of the room.

'Ali's been sick over Tina's best dress, and Semra has lost her great-grandmother's locket.'

Miss Vicars threw up her hands.

'Why do mothers send their kids to school wearing their best clothes and family heirlooms? There should be a law against it! Have you had a good search for the locket?'

'The classroom's been turned inside out. We've done nothing else since lunch.'

'I shall be glad myself when this week's over,' said Sally, handing round the coffee. 'How long is it to the summer break?'

'Four weeks, one day and seventy minutes,' was Gwen's prompt reply, and even Jeanette had to laugh.

'I'm certainly ready for it,' she owned. 'I never felt tired like this at home.'

'But then you didn't teach the little ones.' Miss Vicars fitted a cigarette into a long holder. 'There's a lot to be said for teaching the older children; they're much less wearing.'

'You can say that again!' Sally grimaced. 'I seem to be spending most of my time tying shoelaces, wiping noses and trying to teach the little – angels that my name's not "Mummy".'

A few minutes before the end of afternoon school Gwen came into Jeanette's classroom.

'Are you feeling any better?' she asked, examining her friend's pallid face with concern.

'Not really.'

'Don't you want to come tonight, then?'

'Oh, yes; I shall be all right when I've had a rest.' They had all been invited to a birthday party, after which they were to go on to a night club to hear the famous folk singer, Rubi Su, who owned the club. 'I'll lie down for a while when I get home. It doesn't start till nine, you said?'

'That's right. Don't worry about transport. If I don't pick you up myself I'll arrange for Çetin to do so.'

Despite her optimism Jeanette felt no better by eight o'clock, when it was time to get ready for the party. Her head ached and her legs felt weak as she rose from the couch where she had been lying. A bath would probably help, she decided, and was about to go upstairs when Craig appeared at the window. She crossed the room to open it for him; he had just come along to return a book of Mark's, he explained, stepping inside.

'He isn't in yet,' she told him. 'I think that both he and Tony must be detained at the university; they sometimes are.'

Craig seemed not to have heard. He was scanning her face critically.

'Are you unwell?' he asked, frowning. He sounded anxious, she thought, then dismissed the idea as absurd.

'Not really – just tired.' She managed a faint smile. 'It's been a trying week.'

'Let me look at you.' He tilted her face to examine it more closely. 'Hmm . . . I see.' Jeanette formed the impression that he had made a diagnosis and was greatly relieved by it. 'You'd better go to bed, at once, and if you stay at home tomorrow and rest you should be all right.'

The authoritative manner in which he had assumed control of the situation both startled and annoyed her, and her voice held a hint of defiance when she spoke.

'I can't go to bed; I'm going out.'

'Out?' He looked amazed. 'Is it imperative that you go out?'

Angry colour rose to her face. Why he should take it upon himself to interfere was beyond her comprehension. The fact of his being her brother's friend in no way entitled him to do so – though probably he had the presumption to think it did.

'Yes, as a matter of fact, it is.' She spoke with more control than she thought possible. 'I promised.'

'Where are you going?' he demanded in tones edged with irritation. 'It can't be that important!'

'To a party!' she flashed, on a challenging note.

There was an astounded silence before Craig said, very softly,

'You can't be serious?'

Jeanette's eyes fell before the scathing glance he gave her. He had implied that her conduct was irrational and of course he was right. She felt so weak that, had he used a little diplomacy, a little persuasion, she would willingly – even gratefully – have done as he recommended. As it was, his autocratic manner impelled her to make it quite clear that he had no control whatsoever over her actions.

'I am serious,' she said, then added sarcastically, 'I'm sorry you don't approve—'

'I absolutely for—' He broke off, obviously aware that he went too far. 'Try to use your sense,' he amended. 'You're not fit to go out, and you're well aware of it!'

She bit her lip in vexation at his reading of her thoughts, and at the same time wished fervently that he had not adopted this high-handed manner which goaded her into a resistance which was sheer folly. Argument with him was a strain; it would be much more comfortable to let him have his own way, but her pride fought against submission.

'I intend to go out,' she stated. 'If you'll excuse me, I shall have to get ready.' At the door she turned. 'Perhaps you'd rather not wait? I don't know how long—'

'I'll wait!' he snapped, and then, 'How are you getting to this place?'

There was a slight hesitation that was not lost on him before she replied,

'Someone is calling for me.' And as he made no further comment she turned and left the room, hoping it would be Gwen, and not Çetin, who came to fetch her.

Recalling that Craig had been about to use the word 'forbid', Jeanette derived extreme satisfaction from his having been forced to check himself. Used as he was to giving orders, it must be a new and galling experience for him to have his will opposed.

On returning to the sitting-room she found him standing by the window, gazing out across the strait. Tall and erect, with his profile outlined darkly in the dimmed and softened light from a single wall lamp, he presented a grim and forbidding figure. Jeanette was suddenly reminded of what Gwen had once said of him. 'I've only met Craig Fleming a couple of times, but he strikes me as being cold as the marble gods he digs up!'

He turned, his eyes flickering over her indifferently.

'Çetin called for you,' he calmly informed her. 'I sent him away.'

'You—' She stared at him incredulously. 'Wh-what did you say?'

'I think you heard me. I told him to make your apologies.'

She could hardly speak. Anger almost suffocated her and nothing would have given her greater satisfaction than to tell him exactly what she thought of him, but, as always, she had to remember that he was her brother's friend. To quarrel with him might not actually produce a rift, but it must assuredly impair the easy relationship which existed between the two men.

Her anger turned to mortification at the idea of his having defeated her, after all, but at the same time what little strength she had left seemed to desert her and she could only murmur feebly,

'You had no right to send him away. . . .' Moving to the couch, she sat down, becoming rather frightened. Could she be sickening for some obscure eastern disease?

'If you don't go upstairs at once you'll not manage it alone,' Craig warned her calmly. Then, with a hint of bitterness, 'I'm sure, in your present mood, you would hate the idea of my having to carry you.'

He left her then, and went in search of Mrs. Baydur. Within ten minutes Jeanette was slipping between the sheets, glad to be in bed and admitting, with a slight sense of shock, that it was most pleasant to be managed, and wishing she had followed Craig's advice in the first place. He had gone home, but after a while she heard his voice again. As he entered the room without even knocking she assumed he had inquired of the housekeeper if she were in bed.

'Sit up and drink this,' he ordered, holding out the glass. Jeanette took it, and pulled a face.

'It smells horrid – and it might not do me any good. After all, you don't know what's wrong with me.'

'Certainly I know what's wrong with you. Now drink it.'

She obeyed, eyeing him questioningly.

'I thought it was the children – that they had exhausted me, but I'm so *physically* tired!'

'You're quite literally under the weather,' explained Craig with a faint smile. 'You've been badly affected by the *odos* wind.' He paused as her eyes widened in surprise. 'This wind blows up from the south and has a strange effect on some people; it makes them lethargic, saps their vitality. Certain people are more severely affected than others – it had an almost paralysing effect on my grand-mother, and she was used to it. It even affects the fish,' he added, and Jeanette's eyes became suspicious. 'I'm quite serious,' he said, ignoring her glance. 'It makes them slow in movement.'

'But there's often a southerly wind,' she pointed out, 'and it's never before made me feel like this.'

'Every southerly wind is not the *odos*. This particular climatic phenomenon is less frequent, which is just as well,' he added, smiling down at her.

'It certainly has brought me low,' she admitted wryly. 'Does it not affect you?'

'At times, yes. That's why I can recognize the symptoms.'

By now Jeanette was entering into that pleasant state bordering on slumber and suspected the draught given her by Craig had something to do with it. On an apologetic note she informed him that she could no longer keep her eyes open.

'Good. Now remember, rest tomorrow, otherwise there'll be no attending the Queen's Birthday celebra-tions for you on Saturday.'

'I'm n-not g-going. ...' Everyone she knew had received

an invitation, but Jeanette herself had somehow been overlooked, much to her disappointment. Vaguely she knew she was telling Craig about it, and then her eyes pricked and she hovered on the very edge of sleep. From a long distance she heard him saying he was allowed to take a guest . . . and after that she heard no more.

CHAPTER THREE

By the following afternoon Jeanette was already feeling better and she came downstairs to take the opportunity of a few hours in the garden with a book. But it lay unopened in her lap as she gazed dreamily across the strait. The Bosphorus, stirred by the swift current moving from the Black Sea to the Sea of Marmara, reflected the shapes and colours of the overhanging buildings in a grotesque yet singularly fascinating manner. As usual the Bosphorus surged with life. Busy water traffic passed to and fro; the familiar *kayiks*, the car and passenger ferries plying between Usküar, Istanbul and Kadioköy. The larger vessels from distant parts of the world, the yachts and other pleasure craft on their way across the Sea of Marmara to the Princes' Islands. On days like this the Asiatic shore seemed so close that the cottages, suspended on the hillsides, seemed almost to be within calling distance.

A soft peace pervaded the garden, with only the occasional insect drone to disturb the silence. The silence itself became so soothing that Jeanette drifted into the daydreams of half-sleep and back again many times. Dominating these misty visions was the image of Craig Fleming in all his changing moods – now curt and aloof, now smiling and friendly, now cold with anger and impatience.

She recalled that first month, when his avoidance of her seemed planned and deliberate. It was as though he had resolved, almost as soon as she arrived, to keep her at a distance. Since Ned's death she had been rather pampered; people had gone out of their way to be kind. Craig's attitude was new, and strangely hurtful. Moreover, it undermined her confidence so that conversation with him had become difficult. Then the sudden and surprising interest, beginning on the evening he had taken the walk with her, and the subsequent sightseeing trip when constraint between them was replaced by an intimacy of which she at least had been profoundly conscious. Lastly, and most surprising of all, was the coercive, arbitrary manner of last evening. That was not the conduct of a mere acquaintance, but rather that of one whose authority had some basis, one with an established right to question her actions.

Languid with warmth and drowsiness, Jeanette closed her eyes. All very puzzling . . . but not really important. . . .

She sat up with a welcoming smile as she heard footsteps on the gravel and Gwen came round the corner of the patio.

'How does the invalid feel now?' Gwen dropped to the grass beside Jeanette's chair. 'Better, I see.'

'Much, thank you. How are things at school? Did my absence cause much inconvenience?'

'The Head took your class – do her good to suffer the strain of teaching again!'

'You enjoy every minute of it!' Jeanette laughed.

'I suppose I do, but it's so tiring. It must be the heat of this place.'

'We're lucky, you know, being paid for something we love doing. Not everyone feels so happy in his job.' She picked up her book and dropped it absently on to the grass. 'I feel a fraud sitting here, just lazing about.'

'You needn't. I've been brought down like it myself. The moment Çetin mentioned it I realized I should have known. The fact was, we all thought you were sickening for hepatitis.'

Recalling the way Craig had examined her face Jeanette knew that he too had considered the possibility.

'Çetin gave you the message, then?' Jeanette spoke in tones of faint embarrassment. 'Did you make my apologies to Teresa?'

Gwen nodded.

'Çetin was most put out by the way Craig Fleming treated him.'

'Oh,' was all Jeanette could find to say as the colour rose in her cheeks.

'According to Çetin he had taken complete command of the situation – adopted a most dictatorial attitude, in fact.' Jeanette fixed her eyes with great intentness on a bush of pink oleanders splashing their colour against the green of the smooth wide lawn. It occurred to her that Craig had probably shown actual rudeness towards Çetin, considering his unconcealed dislike of the handsome young Turk. Certainly his handling of the situation must seem very odd to all who knew of it, but Jeanette could find nothing to say either in explanation or excuse. 'Craig appears to have taken a sudden interest in you,' remarked Gwen when Jeanette made no response. 'According to those who know him well he's never had much time for women.'

'He probably feels he should show a little interest in me,' said Jeanette, managing to meet Gwen's curious gaze, 'because of his friendship with Mark.' She thought about Craig's offer to take her to the Consulate function tomorrow and decided she had better mention it to Gwen, for both she and Sally knew Jeanette had not been invited and would, therefore, not be expecting to see her there. Her friend's eyes opened wide at this information and Jeanette's colour deepened. However, Gwen made no further remarks about Craig, and the conversation became less personal, much to Jeanette's relief.

Jeanette awoke the next morning feeling so fatigued that she began to have doubts about being able to attend the function after all. But as on the previous day she improved as the morning wore on and by lunch time she was up and about, her mind dwelling one moment on the celebrations and the next on the pleasant prospect of having Craig for an escort.

The celebrations were to begin at five in the afternoon and end at seven in the evening. Craig was calling for her at a quarter past four and at three o'clock she went upstairs to wash and dress.

Already laid out on the bed was the outfit – the dusty pink suit with blue accessories and the wide-brimmed hat trimmed with ribbon and net. She had brought it from home with such an occasion as this in mind. Excitement caused her pulse to quicken. Would Craig like it ...? Turning away into the bathroom, she forced a strict discipline upon herself. Craig loved Diane and she, Jeanette, had vowed always to cherish the memory of Ned. Thoughts like this of Craig were not only disloyal to Ned's memory, but they were also futile. Craig belonged to Diane.

After taking a shower, she returned to the bedroom, excitement again surging over her despite her determined efforts at control. She put on the skirt and began to zip up. The next moment she was staring down at it, aghast. The zip fastener had broken.

'What can I do?' She was almost in tears, for there was nothing else suitable for this particular occasion. 'I can't go. ...' Her disappointment became so acute that she was forced to speculate on it for a moment or two. She had been disappointed at not receiving an invitation, naturally, because her brother and her friends had been invited – but she hadn't felt so bitterly disappointed as this.

With a frantic little gesture she opened her wardrobe and began a thorough search among her clothes for a substitute. One dress only might do – an expensive and exquisitely cut turquoise linen bought at the last moment and so there had been no time to buy a hat or accessories. She had white shoes and gloves, and a small white handbag. ...

Ten minutes later she was in the sitting-room, standing before Tony, telling him that she couldn't possibly go to the Consulate function.

'The dress is too plain – it needs something to relieve it. It doesn't look right; you can see that, can't you?' Despite her emphatic assertion that she couldn't attend the function because she wasn't suitably dressed, Jeanette

47

waited hopefully for a word of reassurance.

Unused to the ways of women, Tony looked her over, hesitated and said,

'Well . . . perhaps it isn't quite right. . . .'

'What do you mean by that?' she demanded. He was sitting on the arm of a chair, immaculate in light grey linen. She cast him a plaintive glance and he moved uncomfortably, as if it was his fault she hadn't the correct accessories. 'It will have to do,' she groaned. 'I haven't a necklace or a brooch and I can't go wandering about looking for something. It'll be bad enough asking Craig to stop while I buy a hat—'

'What!' Tony jerked up straight and shot her a glance of disbelief. 'You're not going to stop on the way to buy a hat?'

'Why not? It won't take many minutes.'

A sceptical light entered Tony's eyes.

'You can say that again! My sister's husband was once misguided enough to go with her to buy a hat. He talks about it to this very day. No, Jeanette, Craig won't stand for that sort of caper.'

'What do you mean by caper?' she demanded hotly. 'Anyone would think buying a hat is a major operation.'

'Isn't it?'

She bit her lip.

'Don't you think he will agree?'

'I'm darned sure he won't!'

'Tony, how can you be so unfeeling?' she wailed. 'You make it sound as if it's an unheard of thing. Craig won't mind stopping for five minutes.'

'Five minutes?' he ejaculated, and she did have the grace to blush. 'Come, Jeanette, it's too much to ask of any man.' He paused. 'You must have a hat of some sort that would do. What about that pretty green one you wear?'

She stared at him in amazement.

'Green with turquoise?' Jeanette stopped, listening.

48

'He's here. Tony, what am I to do? I just can't go, that's all.'

Metat opened the door and Craig entered; Jeanette did not at first see the small box he carried, for she was anxiously searching his face, speculating on his mood and wondering if she dared venture to make her request.

His glance flickered over her and came to rest on her face. She was flushed and her lips trembled with disappointment. She said, with a gesture of resignation,

'I can't go, Craig, you see—' She stopped. It sounded ridiculous to say she couldn't go when she was standing there, presumably waiting for him to come and fetch her.

'Anything wrong?' His dark eyes strayed to Tony, who suddenly grinned – and told Craig what had happened.

'Tony!' Jeanette's colour deepened; Craig smiled in some amusement and began to untie the ribbon securing the box.

'You look . . . charming.' He meant it, too, no doubt of that. Jeanette watched as he took out the orchid and dropped the box on to a chair. 'I bought it for your hair, but – Hold your head up.' He gave her no time to do so, but lifted it himself. After pinning the flower on to her dress he stood back. 'Yes, much more attractive there than in your hair.'

Jeanette stared up at him, her colour no longer caused by embarrassment.

'You bought it for my hair? But what about my hat?'

'No hats. Didn't I mention that the Consul-General had specially requested that the ladies wouldn't wear hats?'

'No hats?' Tony threw back his head and roared with laughter; Jeanette cast him a darkling glance and his mirth subsided at once. 'All right – all right, I won't say a word.'

Craig, puzzled, looked from one to the other, but when neither proffered any explanation of Tony's sudden outburst he returned his attention to Jeanette, the smile reappearing as he looked her over appreciatively.

'Yes, it's just right on your dress. Your hair needs no adornment.'

Putting up a hand to finger the soft petals, Jeanette smiled and thanked him. Tony coughed discreetly as if to remind them of his presence and Craig's tones became abrupt as he said it was time they were on their way.

They were just going out when Mark came downstairs. The two men greeted each other and then Craig said,

'Mother's here, and Diane; they arrived this morning.

Diane.... Jeanette's heart fluttered.

'This is sudden ... you weren't expecting them?' Mark's eyes flickered strangely, searching Craig's face.

'Hadn't the faintest idea they were coming, but you know Mother. This isn't the first time she's descended upon me without warning. I believe she makes up her mind on the spur of the moment and then hops on the first available plane.'

'But Diane – why is she here?'

'She's been suffering from strain lately – Mother has mentioned it once or twice – and the doctor became worried about her. He had a word with Roy, saying she needed a change and a rest. Roy insisted on her taking a holiday. Apparently Mother was already contemplating one of her flying visits to me, so she suggested Diane come with her.'

'How long are they staying?'

'About a week. Roy has a nurse, as you know, but Diane won't leave him for long.'

'But a week ... it's hardly worth coming for.'

'I agree – and Diane can't possibly derive much benefit from it. I shall try to persuade her to stay for at least another week, but I doubt whether she will.' He shrugged resignedly and changed the subject, glancing quickly at his watch.

'It's time we were all on our way.' A slight pause. 'You're quite sure you and Tony don't want a lift?'

Mark shook his head.

'No, Craig, thanks. As I said, we prefer to go in my

car so that we can come away when we feel like it.'

'Craig—' Jeanette stopped by the car and turned. 'If you would rather not go I won't mind at all. I'm sure you'd prefer to be at home with your mother and – and your friend.' Disappointment began to flood over her again, but she managed to smile up at Craig. 'You didn't know they were coming when you offered to take me – and if you're going merely because of that promise. . . .'

'Get in Jeanette; we're going to be late.' Murad was waiting, the car door open; putting a firm hand under her arm Craig urged her into the back seat, then took his place beside her.

'If they're only here for a week,' Jeanette persisted, certain that he must be regretting his promise, 'they'll want you to be with them. It isn't very nice for your friend after coming all this way.'

'Diane won't mind; she and Mother get on fine. Besides, it isn't very long – we'll be back again just after seven.' Murad closed the door and slid into the driver's seat. The car began to move away. 'You'll meet them both tonight at the Hilton. I rang as soon as they arrived and reserved a larger table.'

'Am I going to the Hilton?' She stared at him in surprise, and a faint smile curved his lips.

'We're all going. Didn't Mark tell you?'

Jeanette shook her head.

'For dinner?'

'Yes.' His smile was faintly mocking. 'I arranged it; I hope you don't mind?' He leant back as if to see her face more clearly. They had reached the end of the drive and were soon purring along the Ortaköy Caddesi, following the shores of the Bosphorus.

'Why should I mind?' ventured Jeanette after a small silence.

'I seem to remember you object to being . . . managed.' A smile quivered; she turned to him impulsively.

'I'm sorry about that, Craig. Was I very – horrid?'

'Very. But I'll excuse it because you were ill.'

Her glance fluttered uncertainly. She sought for some sign of amusement or indulgence in his expression, but his face was a mask – cool, impassive.

'As a matter of fact, it was a relief to be managed.' Most pleasant, too, but Jeanette did not mention that to Craig.

'Was it, Jeanette?' He turned a quizzical glance upon her. 'I shall remember that.'

To Jeanette's surprise the Queen's official birthday celebrations were for the most part an informal affair. Familiar with the routine, Craig took her arm and led her into the main entrance of the Consulate, through the spectacular palm court with its domed roof, its tropical plants and marble statuary.

After being welcomed by the Consul-General and his wife, who were on the steps awaiting the guests, Jeanette and Craig went out on to the lawn. Craig seemed to know everyone and Jeanette found herself shaking hands with managers and representatives from many famous firms in the United Kingdom.

Then they sat at a table in the shade of the trees, eating and drinking and 'socializing'. Several managers of other oil companies had joined them and they chatted for a while and then a hush descended as, over the loudspeaker, came the announcement that the Consul-General would now propose the toast to Her Majesty. The toast was followed by the National Anthem, then the Turkish National Anthem. There followed more socializing and a little while later the guests began to drift away.

'Well, did it come up to your expectations?' Craig asked with a smile as they drove from the Consulate.

'I thought it would be more formal,' she returned vaguely. 'I don't really know what I expected. But I thoroughly enjoyed it. Thank you for taking me, Craig.'

'Don't thank me, Jeanette. I enjoyed taking you.'

She glanced swiftly at him, struck by his tone. He sounded so sincere – and yet Jeanette knew that his entire thoughts must be with Diane, that he must be impatient to be home and with her.

'I'll see you later,' Craig said when he dropped her off. 'You'll be going along with Mark and Tony; we're all meeting at about eight o'clock at the hotel.'

Craig was already there when Jeanette's party arrived, he and Diane were dancing, and after Mark had introduced her to Craig's mother Jeanette found herself scanning the floor, searching for Craig and his partner. They were not difficult to find, for Craig's tall, lithe figure would have stood out anywhere. They drew near . . . and Jeanette caught her breath. No wonder Mark had said people used to turn and stare! Never had she seen a more attractive couple; both so distinguished, both so incredibly good-looking.

Diane was laughing up at Craig, a soft smile curving her lips. Craig's dark eyes held affection and to Jeanette it seemed that his smile portrayed a great depth of tenderness.

During the meal Craig's whole attention was with his visitors and as Tony and Mark became immersed in their own discussion Jeanette had no choice but to withdraw from the conversation. Mrs. Fleming's affection for her future daughter-in-law was evident all the time, in the way she looked at Diane, in the way she spoke and smiled. Now and then she would pass some remark to Jeanette, but it was clearly for the sake of politeness, her interest the whole time being concentrated on Diane and Craig. Diane, herself a charming woman, attracted a considerable amount of attention from men at the nearby tables. Her hair, dark and shining, was the sort that every girl envied, completely natural with no sign that a hairdresser had touched it. Her skin, pale and clear, required no artificial aid to enhance its beauty. She had a soft and husky voice and an adorable smile. No wonder the male heads turned! But Diane remained aloof, neither flattered nor disconcerted. It was easy to see why Craig was so in love with her.

Eventually he took her off to dance again and Jeanette's

53

eyes followed them. Sometimes Diane would look up to give Craig that enchanting smile. What was his reaction? Jeanette felt his pulses must be racing, that he sighed inwardly, impatient for the day when they could be together always. A little ache plucked at her heart. It was impossible that she could envy Diane, and yet what was this emotion? – this strange yearning that had come to her the moment she saw Craig and Diane together?

She tried to divert her attention to the other dancers, aware of some inner voice warning her of the essential need to combat this persistent intrusion of Craig into her thoughts. But her eyes were drawn to them again, following them with a pensive, brooding expression. How happy they were, Craig holding her close and Diane looking so absurdly young – and acting that way too. As for Craig, he also seemed younger and much more relaxed than Jeanette had ever imagined he could be. They came close; Craig practically stopped, looking down at Diane and wagging an admonitory finger at her. His eyes had assumed a severity; he appeared to be threatening her.

With laughter in her eyes but mock protest in her voice Diane exclaimed,

'I believe you would! But I'll do as I'm told, Craig, I promise.'

'You'd better,' grimly. 'We don't want you having a breakdown. Take more care, do you hear?'

'Yes ... I have promised.' Her tone was submissive, but then she added, 'You're going to make a horrid, domineering husband—' Jeanette heard no more, for Craig swung Diane away, out of earshot. The next moment their laughter floated across to Jeanette.

Yes, they were young again, sweethearts playing the love game – snatching back, for a brief spell, a little of what they had lost.

Mark and Tony had gone off to find partners and Jeanette was alone with Mrs. Fleming who had also been listening to the conversation between Diane and her son, for she gave a deep sigh and asked Jeanette if she knew about Roy, Diane's husband, and about his illness.

'Mark told me. It's very sad.'

'Sad for Roy? He could have fared much worse. He was lucky to marry Diane.' Regret in the voice, but more than that, Jeanette noticed; a hint of anger, yes, and bitterness too. Clearly she considered her son had been cheated. 'Roy is good and generous – but he's robbed poor Diane of her youth.'

Jeanette began to feel uncomfortable and it was a relief when Mark appeared and asked her to dance. She slipped into his arms feeling slightly comforted, but a chill had crept over her and the rest of the evening dragged. Craig danced with her once, but his manner was casual, and she felt sure he had asked her merely because it was the polite thing to do.

She was at the buffet with Mark when Craig and Diane came to join them. Mark eventually took Diane off to dance and Jeanette turned to watch them. They, too, made a handsome pair, she thought, her attention suddenly diverted as she became aware of Craig's expression as he, too, watched the departing couple. His eyes were glinting strangely. Surely he wasn't jealous of her brother?

He turned to regard Jeanette, but in an abstracted sort of way, his thoughts appearing to be still engaged with Mark and Diane. He remained thoughtful for a long while, but when at last he spoke his interest had turned wholly to Jeanette.

'Tired?'

Did she look so awful? Diane would never look tired ... or miserable. Jeanette forced a smile.

'A little,' she admitted, 'and hot. It's stifling in here.'

'That at least can be remedied. We'll go outside.'

They stood on the balcony; beneath them the Bosphorus scintillated with stars, lights from the flickering lanterns of numberless fishing craft.

'This is better. Did you notice the heat, too?'

He nodded.

'Especially when I danced.' He fell silent as though content with the stillness and the peace. But to Jeanette the silence was a strain; her nerves quivered and she was torn between an instinct to return indoors and a longing to remain alone with Craig. Awkwardness assailed her; she moved restlessly. Was it owing to Diane's presence here that she felt so ill at ease? She had had Craig's attention all to herself on several occasions recently; being escorted by him had given her confidence, but now. . . .

Craig turned to watch a launch speeding towards Marmara and when he turned again he came close to her, much closer than before. In other circumstances the manoeuvre could have been deliberately planned, but Jeanette knew his nearness was accidental, that Craig himself was totally unaware of it. But it affected her profoundly; she was moved by fear, an exquisite, throbbing fear that left her heart and mind in tumult. Abruptly she edged away . . . and sensed the change in him.

'Shall we go in and join the others?' His voice was crisp and hard. Her lips trembled; she heard again the soft and gentle tones he used when talking to Diane.

'If – if you wish.' Her voice must sound flat and dejected; she wondered if he were bored.

'It isn't what I wish, Jeanette,' came the sharp and unexpected retort. 'You complained of the heat, and I suggested we come out here for a breath of air, but now you seem restless. Would you rather go inside again?'

Silence. She had no idea what she wanted; in any case, the words stuck in her throat; she could not speak in face of such impatience. She stared unseeingly at the lights, flickering on the Asiatic shore across the strait; she was only half aware of the scented air, soft as thistledown, and the whisper of breeze stirring her hair.

'Perhaps it's been a little too much for you,' said Craig in rather gentler tones. 'We'll see if Mark will take you home.'

Mark was already approaching, with Diane.

'It's too crowded for comfort, and much too hot.' Diane

caught Craig's arm possessively, and then let go of it again. 'Oh, I'm sorry— Did I interrupt anything?'

'No, dear, you didn't interrupt anything. Jeanette is just going home – if Mark will take her?' He looked questioningly at his friend. 'If not, then I will. I can always come back.'

'Are you tired?' Diane spoke with concern, looking at Jeanette's face. 'Craig tells me you've been ill.'

'It was nothing, really.' Jeanette's glance flickered up to Craig. It surprised her that he should have discussed her indisposition with Diane. Mark was stating his willingness to take her home, saying that Tony was also ready to go and Jeanette had no choice but to agree to Craig's suggestion. After the good nights had been said she turned away with Mark; Diane took Craig's arm again and Jeanette half jerked her head to see them standing there, close together, looking up at the eastern sky with its lace of cloud unfolding, drifting apart in shreds to reveal the pearl-tinted heavens and a moon cut through by the peak of a distant height across on the Asiatic shore. Diane's head moved to one side, coming to rest against her companion's shoulder.

CHAPTER FOUR

APPARENTLY Diane wanted to explore the city, and a little of the surrounding countryside, visiting the main places of interest. Craig, on the other hand, was insisting she take things easy. A compromise was eventually reached. Craig would agree to the sightseeing only if Diane would first of all spend a few days on Büyük Ada, taking a complete rest.

Having been invited to dinner, along with her brother and Tony, Jeanette sat at Craig's candlelit table and listened silently to the lighthearted argument taking place between Craig and Diane.

'It means you'll have to stay for more than a week,' he said, attentively applying himself to Diane's needs.

'But, Roy, he—'

'Will not mind in the least,' interposed Craig's mother eagerly. 'He said himself that it was silly to come all this way for only one week. There's no real reason why we can't stay longer, Diane dear. He'll be quite all right with the nurse.'

'Very well,' Diane agreed only after a rather lengthy consideration and then, 'Jeanette tells me she has two days' holiday at the beginning of next week and as Mark and Tony are also on holiday, we could make a party. Can we, Craig?' She gave him one of her most adorable smiles and although Craig did hesitate, it was only momentarily.

'That would be fine. I had no idea you were on holiday next week, Jeanette.'

'It's just a short half-term break. We have to be in on Wednesday.' Jeanette watched his expression, unable to decide wether he really welcomed the idea of extra guests, or wether he just couldn't refuse Diane anything she wanted.

'We can come back on Tuesday, then?' Although Diane looked questioningly at Craig, her tone suggested the matter was settled. He nodded, and asked Tony and Mark how they were fixed, and if they had already made arrangements for the holiday. Neither had, and it was decided they should sail for the island on Friday evening.

The Bosphorus was as smooth as glass, glowing like fire as the sun dropped behind the hills; not a breath of wind stirred the surface, and Craig said they would have to use the engine.

They came out of the strait, to glide smoothly across the Sea of Marmara. Jeanette looked back to see lights springing up all over the city and the beautiful silhouette of St. Sophia outlined against the deepening sky, with its four minarets rising heavenwards.

Then she became aware of the sparks raining all over the sea around them, and of the wake shining with a strange brilliance, streaming a long way behind and seeming never to disappear.

'What is it?' she asked in a slightly awed voice as Craig, having left Mark in control, came and stood beside her.

'Phosphorescence,' he explained. 'Surely you've noticed it before? Look out for the porpoises – See!' She watched, fascinated, as the playful creatures sent their arcs of light shooting across the water; the tracks remained long after the fish had disappeared. 'You get it whenever anything touches the water. We anchor the yacht sometimes and swim – when the moon is full – and our movements have the same effect.' More porpoises came close and Jeanette held her breath, sure they would be hit. 'It's a pity there's no wind,' Craig commented, his glance sweeping the still water around them. 'I much prefer to sail.'

They saw several small islands, all part of the Princes' Islands group, and at last reached Büyük Ada – the 'Big Island'.

Gay cafés along the quay lighted the waterfront, their glow mingling with a million stars shining from an eastern sky and reflected in the dark and placid waters of Marmara.

The population of Büyük Ada was mainly Greek; unlike the Turks, they possessed a natural gaiety which imparted an air of abandon to the island. It was first and foremost a holiday island, though whole families of wealthy Turks and Greeks would move out from the city to spend the summer months there. Craig commented on its growing popularity, with its consequent overcrowding at this time of the year. Had he been intending to settle in Turkey he would have moved to Heybeli, which was less crowded and not nearly so expensive as Büyük Ada.

The *yali* was charming, having been renovated and furnished with an eye to comfort as well as taste, yet it still retained its eastern atmosphere for, structurally, it was in its original state, constructed entirely of wood, with heavily latticed windows and the characteristic overhanging upper storeys.

Tony and Mark had of course seen it all before, and so had Craig's mother, but the two girls were thrilled and intrigued. Diane, with her usual confidence, went around touching everything, and commenting on it, while Jeanette just stood staring at a tapestry that almost covered one wall. Craig came and stood behind her.

'Recognize it?' he asked, and she nodded. His hands dropped on to her shoulders; it was a friendly, automatic gesture, but she quivered under his touch. Had he noticed? Swiftly, she began to speak.

'Topkapi – the Seraglio; the plane trees and flowers – the kiosks and – and of course, the mosques and minarets in the background. . . .' Jeanette swallowed hard, praying fervently that her confusion would pass unnoticed by Craig.

Arrested, Diane came and joined them. After examining the tapestry for a moment in silence she turned to smile up mischievously at Craig.

'The ladies of the harem, I take it?' she observed. 'You surprise me, Craig.'

'Can't see anything wrong,' interposed Mark, turning. 'All very decent – ladies fully clothed, and one or two even yashmaked. Quite prudish, in fact. I've seen some I'd like better,' he added, grinning.

'I bought it for the workmanship, mainly,' said Craig in quiet thoughtful tones and then, 'Tell me, Jeanette, what impresses you most about the scene?'

A long hesitation; Jeanette felt her answer would arouse only surprised amusement.

'It's the cards,' she murmured awkwardly.

'The cards?' Diane frowned and looked at the pack of playing cards scattered about on the exquisitely tiled floor of the courtyard. 'What do you mean?'

'I think I know.' The slight pressure of Craig's hands on Jeanette's shoulders could almost have been a subtle way of expressing his satisfaction at her reply. 'They have been tossed down, and demonstrate, very forcibly, I think, just how bored those women were.' Jeanette nodded and he went on, 'They're weary of their game – and here you have one smoking a cigarette, another a hookah, while here you have another woman standing over the samovar, making tea. The cards on the floor give the clue as to why these other activities are taking place. It's impressive and beautifully done. I liked it and just had to buy it.'

'Yes, I see it now,' Diane owned, wonderingly. 'It's fascinating, Craig ... and look at the bored expressions on the faces of all the other women. What a life!' She laughed up at Craig and again a mischievous light entered her eyes. 'Just imagine being one of three hundred! What would anyone do with three hundred wives?'

'Have a whale of a time, I shouldn't wonder!' exclaimed Mark, at once infected with Diane's laughter.

'Listen who's talking—' It seemed to Jeanette that there was an almost coquettish element in the glance Diane cast at Mark. 'You, who never even look at a woman!'

'I can still use my imagination, I hope!' he retorted, and even Craig had to join in the laughter.

'Whale of a time or not,' he said, his glance straying to Diane, 'one wife would be enough for me.'

'And me,' echoed Mark in suddenly solemn tones. 'Quite enough,' and he turned away, once more to examine the tapestry.

After supper the time was spent out of doors, but soon Diane announced her intention of going to bed. This met with Craig's approval, but his mother seemed disappointed that he and Diane had not gone off somewhere on their own.

'I thought you two would be going for a walk?' She glanced from Diane to Craig. 'It would do you both good – and it's quite early.' She waited hopefully for an agreement, but Diane shook her head.

'There's nothing to stop Craig going for a walk.' She turned to Jeanette, smiling. 'You'll go with him and keep him company, won't you?'

Mrs. Fleming bit her lip in vexation, and a flush rose swiftly to Jeanette's cheeks.

'I – I think I shall go to bed, too,' she began when Craig interrupted her.

'I'm sure you'd enjoy a walk,' and although she was well aware that the prudent course was to refuse, Jeanette smilingly agreed to accompany him.

It was a magical Eastern night, spread with that mystic purple radiance which seems always to hover in a Turkish sky. Tall palms swayed, smudging the skyline and tossing their perfume on to the silent breeze so that it mingled with the intoxicating scent of magnolia which already filled the air.

They wandered along the beach, where the faintly silvered glow from a young moon sprinkled the sea with light and tinted the foam as it came gently in to caress the shore in an almost soundless motion.

Jeanette had never been so profoundly conscious of Craig, had never experienced such turmoil and confusion of mind. Her thoughts dwelt for a space on Diane; she saw her as Craig's wife and became suddenly engulfed in a terrible, unaccountable feeling of despair. She strove to shake it off. Her eyes were drawn irresistibly to Craig, so tall and straight ... so out of reach. This was no time for intimacies, and yet something stronger than herself impelled her to say,

'It's beautiful.... I'm so grateful to you, Craig, for inviting me.' She hesitated. 'I've been dying to come,' she confessed. 'I did so want to see the inside of a *yali*.'

'Then why on earth didn't you say so?' He looked down at her almost angrily. 'You could have come any week-end – the proprieties would have been taken care of,' he added on a slightly sardonic note as he saw her sudden change of expression. 'The couple you saw tonight are here all the time. They look after the place when I'm away.' He took her arm, steering her clear of the wet patch of sand into which she was walking. 'You would be quite safe, I assure you.'

She glanced up in surprise, saw his smile of amusement and laughed lightly.

'I know that, but I wouldn't have dreamed of asking to come. You want privacy, and quietness, in order to work on your book; you told me that right at the beginning.'

'And why should your presence hinder my work?' he wanted to know, still regarding her with that hint of amusement. 'You might have been able to assist me with it.'

'I don't think so,' she returned doubtfully, and was just beginning to wonder once again how much her brother had told Craig about her when he said,

'Mark tells me that you have some considerable knowledge of archaeology—'

'Not considerable,' she broke in, flushing. 'Mark must have exaggerated.'

'But you have done some digging?'

'Yes.'

'And you're conversant with many other aspects of the subject – you've done some editing, I believe?'

She nodded.

'I attended several courses at the university. We had a marvellous lecturer.' She mentioned his name and Craig's eyes widened with interest. He not only knew him, but had worked with him on a wonderful find that had been made in London several years previously.

'Then it seems to me that Mark didn't exaggerate,' he commented, and, unexpectedly, 'Would you care to help me, Jeanette?'

Again that indefinable fear, that warning to steer clear of any intimate relationship with Craig.

'I don't know – you see. . . .'

'Yes?' His dark brows lifted questioningly.

'It's so awkward.'

'Is it, Jeanette?' His tone for a moment was gentle, but then he seemed to lose patience. 'What possible excuse can you have for not coming?'

How could she reveal her excuse? In any case, it was not valid, it had no substance. She was not afraid of Craig – but she was afraid of being alone with him. Could she give that as an excuse? She shook her head miserably.

'I'm sorry, Craig, but I'd rather not.'

A long silence, the silence of anger. When he spoke his voice was brittle.

'If I don't end up by doing you an injury it will be a miracle!' His hand was abruptly withdrawn from her arm; Jeanette stopped, her eyes fluttering as she looked up to meet his darkling gaze. She recalled how he had teasingly threatened Diane . . . but there was nothing teasing in his manner now. Nevertheless, he could not be serious. He probably made the threat as a diversion in order to enjoy her embarrassment. But it seemed he did not want to enjoy her embarrassment, for almost immediately his face softened. 'Very well; forget it if you like, Jeanette, but—' He stood looking down at her, the merest smile touching his lips. 'I would welcome your help; I really mean that.' They began walking along the shore again and, strangely, the silence between them was not in the least constrained. In fact, Jeanette felt oddly happy, and after a little while, forgetful of those inner warnings, she told him that she would like to help him with the book, after all.

'You would? That's fine. When we get back I'll show you what I'm doing – how far I've progressed – and explain what I want. But for the present – would you like some coffee?'

'In one of those little cafés over there? Oh, yes, please!'

Unhurried, and in an atmosphere of harmony and companionship comparable with that which had come to them on the occasion of their visit to Topkapi, they strolled on towards the cafés and the lights.

'Shall we sit outside?' Taking her acceptance for granted, Craig pulled out a chair for her and Jeanette sat down. Life throbbed all around them and Jeanette had that breathless sensation of living in an unreal world, of being somewhere 'off the map'. Just along from them two men sat drinking coffee and smoking *narghiles*, and passing to and fro the whole time were the quaint horse-drawn carriages – for no cars were allowed on the island. Behind them, gardens filled with exotic plants cast seductive perfumes into the breeze; and away on the far horizon a ship's lights flickered, golden points standing out in the star-filled sky.

'What are you dreaming of?' asked Craig as Jeanette, sipping her coffee, gazed pensively into space. A smile spread and she put down her cup.

'I was thinking that I'm lucky – really being here and seeing all this.'

Craig's eyes followed a passing carriage; he watched it disappear from sight.

'Why the "really"? What does it mean?'

'It was just a – figure of speech.'

'No, Jeanette, it wasn't that. Can't you tell me?'

For some reason Jeanette felt sure he was making a subtle reference to Ned, and now she knew that Mark had discussed her misfortune with Craig, telling him all about it. Had he mentioned, too, her resolve never to marry? — to remain faithful to Ned's memory? She thought he must have done ... and now Craig was being sympathetic. He was showing interest, willing to take on the role of father confessor. Strangely, though, she hadn't been thinking of Ned. With a feeling of consternation and guilt she realized that his memory had become dimmer and dimmer. Even his image had faded; she couldn't see his face. Almost frantically she tried to bring it into focus, and failed. To love so deeply and then forget! How wrong it was. Would Ned have forgotten? Jeanette felt sure he would have remembered her for ever, had the positions been reversed. She met Craig's gaze, saw the gravity there, and the inquiring little lift of his brows as he waited patiently for her reply. He it was who had caused her thoughts to stray, but although she made a determined effort to rekindle that first unreasoning resentment against him, she found it quite impossible.

A tremulous little smile came to her lips as she said, on a distinctly apologetic note, that there was nothing to tell. He stiffened slightly and her heart sank. But she could not bring herself to talk of Ned.

Had Craig not been in love with Diane it would have been so easy; but he was in love with Diane, and although his concern appeared to be very real, Jeanette felt that the likelihood of his being genuinely interested in the affairs of another woman must be extremely remote.

'Shall we go, then?'

She nodded, looking up at him unhappily as they moved from the gaily-lighted café into the darkness. The breeze had freshened; automatically she brushed a hand through her hair as it flicked on to her face. It was a dejected little movement and to her surprise Craig sensed it immediately. He drew her arm through his and although he did not speak she derived a strange comfort from the gesture and from the knowledge of his quick perception.

Mrs. Fleming was sitting alone, reading, when they

arrived back at the *yali*. She glanced up with a slight frown as they entered, and then her eyes moved to the clock on the wall. Jeanette felt like a naughty child who had stayed out late. Her chin lifted and she half turned to look at Craig. A glint had entered his eyes, but his tone held no ill-humour when he spoke.

'Where are the others?'

'In bed. Tony and Mark have just gone up.' She closed her book and laid it aside. 'I expect you're going up now, Jeanette?' Clearly she wanted to have a word alone with her son and Jeanette obligingly said good night and turned to the door.

'Good night.' Craig smiled and opened the door for her. 'It's too late now to show you my work; I'll let you see it tomorrow.' His mother looked up sharply, casting him a glance of interrogation. 'Jeanette is going to assist me with the book,' he obligingly informed her, and opened the door wider for Jeanette to pass through.

'But, Craig, surely you're not going to—' Jeanette heard no more; she mounted the stairs slowly, wondering, with a perfectly natural curiosity, what Craig's mother was saying about her. More important perhaps – what was she thinking?

The following afternoon she was given some idea. The men had gone out to tinker with the boat; Diane was in the garden sunbathing, and Jeanette, having come into the house to find her sun-tan lotion, was called into the sitting-room by Mrs. Fleming.

'I just wanted to have a word with you,' she said, in cordial enough tones, but there was a hint of hostility in her clear blue eyes. 'My son tells me you are coming over here at the week-ends to help him with his book?'

'Craig did suggest I do that, yes.'

'Well, my dear, that would hardly be the thing, would it?'

Jeanette eyed her squarely.

'I don't think I understand you, Mrs. Fleming.'

'Does your brother know what you intend doing?'

Mrs. Fleming sat up straight, her manner serene and aloof. Her greying hair was attractively styled, her skin free from lines and glowing with health. She had the aristocratic bearing of her son, with the same proud features and firm set jaw.

'Mark has no authority over my movements,' Jeanette submitted quietly. 'He would never be so presumptuous as to interfere.'

'Perhaps not, but I'm sure, my dear, that it would embarrass him to know that you were spending every week-end over here alone with Craig.'

Jeanette quelled her rising anger; she also had the sense to pause, lest she should on impulse say something she would later come to regret.

'I don't expect to be spending every week-end here, Mrs. Fleming. Craig asked me to help him and I agreed. I can't go back on my word – even if I wanted to.'

'And, I take it, you don't want to.'

'That's correct.'

A slight pause and then,

'I hope, Jeanette, you haven't been so foolish as to fall in love with my son? He's shortly to marry Diane, as you obviously know.'

A deep flush mounted Jeanette's face. The words shocked her; she would never have believed Mrs. Fleming could have asked so blunt a question.

'I have most certainly not fallen in love with your son,' she retorted, her anger still fairly well under control. 'And I assure you, Mrs. Fleming, that there's not the remotest possibility of my doing so.'

Mrs. Fleming's face cleared, but she remained thoughtfully silent, apparently absorbed in the contemplation of a pair of priceless Sèvres vases set on the buhl cabinet under the window.

'Your answer relieves me,' she said at last. 'My son is a most attractive man, and you wouldn't be the first woman to lose her heart—'

'I haven't lost my heart!' Real trouble now with her

temper. Jeanette sought vainly for some excuse to end this conversation.

'No, my dear, you've said so – but I'm merely trying to be kind, to warn you.' She looked her over, from head to foot, and Jeanette gained the extraordinary impression that Mrs. Fleming was making mental comparisons between her and Diane. But why should she do that? The idea was suddenly quite absurd and Jeanette dismissed it from her mind. 'Forgive me, dear, if I've said anything to upset you,' Mrs. Fleming went on in the same cool unhurried tones. 'Perhaps I've been rather outspoken, but my concern for you is genuine. You're a nice girl and I should be most grieved if you were hurt.'

Jeanette at first felt extremely sceptical about this, but as there seemed no reason why Mrs. Fleming should make the statement, unless it were true, she chided herself for her ungenerous thoughts. Nevertheless, she still felt nettled by Mrs. Fleming's assumption that she could be so stupid as to fall in love with her son, knowing as she did that he had waited all these years for Diane.

'You have no need to worry, Mrs. Fleming, I shan't be hurt.'

Instead of returning to the garden, Jeanette went upstairs and changed into a dress; then she went out for a walk, all her pleasurable anticipation of helping Craig crushed under the weight of despair that had begun to settle upon her as the conversation with Mrs. Fleming progressed. Unexpectedly she had been faced with the stark question as to her feelings for Craig, a question which she now knew she'd been persistently avoiding for some time. 'I shan't be hurt', she had told Craig's mother. . . .

She walked and walked, for a long while refusing even to allow the question to come to the forefront of her mind, but eventually she had to admit the truth. Despite all her resolutions to remain faithful to Ned's memory she had fallen irrevocably in love with Craig Fleming.

Tea time had long since passed when Jeanette at length

returned. Diane and the three men were swimming. Mrs. Fleming told her, assuming a rather frigid attitude. She seemed exceedingly hesitant about conveying the message which Craig had left for Jeanette.

'He asked me to say where they were, and tell you to join them as soon as you'd had something to eat.'

'Thank you. I'm not hungry. . . .' She went out again and down the garden to the beach. Craig, lying on the sand with Diane, sat up as she approached and regarded her with a faintly anxious expression.

'Where have you been? We were beginning to think you'd missed your way. In fact, Diane and I have just agreed to go up and change and then come to look for you. Where have you been?' he said again on a curious note.

'Walking.' She forced a smile, conscious that her fists were clenched and that the palms of her hands were damp with sweat. 'I'm sorry about tea, but I forgot the time.'

'Well, so long as you're safe—' Diane sat up, smiling at Jeanette and patting the sand beside her. 'Come and sit down; the air's gorgeous, so balmy and warm.'

'Why didn't you bring your costume?' Craig wanted to know, apparently still curious about Jeanette's prolonged absence from the *yali*. 'I told Mother to tell you we were swimming.'

Jeanette sat down, still smiling; she thought she did very well, considering how she felt.

'I'll not bother to swim now. As a matter of fact I think I'll have an early night – I seem to have tired myself out.'

'No wonder, if you've been walking all this time,' exclaimed Diane. 'I'd be absolutely fagged!'

They sat talking and after a while Tony and Mark joined them. The sun drifted down, tinting the sea, and the brief eastern twilight faded as stars and moon appeared in the purple dome of the sky. Jeanette decided to go indoors, noting as she rose that once again Craig regarded her with that intense and curious expression.

Not long afterwards the others followed, but Jeanette only heard them, for she had already gone to her room.

How long would this last? she wondered as for the second time in her life she felt herself engulfed in black despair. But she would not again sink into the abyss; this time she would fight against her misery. This time it couldn't be so bad, she told herself. Craig had never been hers; she had suffered no actual loss and therefore the hurt couldn't possibly be so great.

She thought about Craig's book, recalling their companionship and the eagerness with which they had discussed it only a few hours earlier. Craig had given her a rough outline of what he wanted her to do; she'd felt confident, and happiness had surged over her as, patting her hand, Craig had said,

'I have every confidence in you, Jeanette. I think we're going to enjoy working together here.'

Well, that was all over even before it had begun. Jeanette tried several times to tell him, but the words stuck in her throat. On the way home, sailing smoothly across the Sea of Marmara, she once again found him standing by her side. This time she made an even greater effort to tell him she had changed her mind, but before she could speak he mentioned her dejection, asking if she was feeling off colour. His anxiety seemed obvious, but Jeanette knew it stemmed merely from politeness. She was his guest and therefore he would feel it incumbent on him to concern himself with her welfare.

'No, I'm fine, thanks, Craig.' She looked up at him and smiled, but he was already shaking his head.

'There's something ... you've been different since Saturday afternoon.' He paused and a grim little smile curved his lips. 'You're an odd child, Jeanette. I wish you'd stop bottling things up.'

'I'm not – not bottling anything up.' His words startled her. What did he mean?

She saw him stiffen; he spoke with that cold politeness which had become so familiar during that first month when he had seemed so determined to keep her at a distance.

'Very well; I shall never again press you to confide in me.'

'Craig! Do come and look at the porpoises; they're so playful!' Diane's voice floated to them from the other side of the boat. With a little shrug which Jeanette felt sure was an indication of his relief, Craig left her and went to join Diane. Jeanette turned away, gazing out to sea. How could she confide in Craig? How could she tell him what was wrong?

Their laughter reached her; the feeling of emptiness drained away, leaving in its place a terrible ache which she knew would be even more difficult to bear. This couldn't go on – what could she do?

Suddenly, as if in answer to a prayer, she recalled that Çetin was taking a party of climbers to explore the curious rock formations in the vicinity of Ulüdağ, near Bursa. Sally and Gwen had at last agreed to join Çetin's party; Jeanette had also been invited, but despite her earlier vow to accept the first offer Çetin made, she had remained undecided, partly owing to Craig's warning, but mainly because of a reluctance to do anything of which Craig would not approve.

Now, she decided, the sensible thing would be to join the party, to go along with her friends and enjoy herself, for only in this way could she ever hope to forget her feelings for Craig.

CHAPTER FIVE

THE rest of Diane's visit was spent between sightseeing and visiting one or two of Craig's friends. Craig himself again invited Jeanette and the two men to dinner, but Jeanette made an excuse and remained at home. Craig also asked Jeanette if she would like to visit Topkapi again. He was taking his mother and Diane on the Saturday, and Jeanette would be very welcome. Again she refused, saying she had promised to go to her friends' flat for the week-end. This was true, for the preparations for the expedition to Ulüdağ were taking place there. These occupied the whole of the week-end, and also much of the following week. Çetin and his two friends, both of whom were Turks, brought their gear to the flat and when Jeanette saw the ropes she experienced some considerable trepidation; nothing so hazardous as the actual tackling of a rock face had entered her mind.

'Are we doing real climbing?' she asked in rather fearful tones. 'I mean – shall we be roped together?'

Çetin was on the floor, tightly rolling up Gwen's sleeping bag.

'Must be, for safety.' Çetin spoke automatically, his whole attention on his task. 'That's about as small as it will go. Now, Sally, where's yours?'

'Mine is tightly rolled. How about yours, Jeanette?'

'It's already strapped to my pack,' she said, suddenly recalling Craig's warning and wondering if it would be wiser to drop out of the expedition. She had somehow thought of the trip as a journey by car, and then the hike, with the added interest of examining the unusual rock formations, but this seemed a major operation, planned systematically down to the last minor detail. No doubt about it, Çetin knew what he was doing.

'He should do,' Sally asserted when Jeanette mentioned

this to her friend as they made coffee in the little kitchen. 'His father is a famous climber. He really does great things.'

By Thursday evening everything was ready; Çetin told them all to be in bed early on Friday night because he intended starting out at dawn on Saturday. Jeanette saw him in a new light. He seemed almost ruthless in his role of organizer; he issued the orders and everyone obeyed. Apparently it was always like this, Gwen informed her, having spoken to others who had joined his climbing parties. He was efficient, but hard.

'You do as you're told whether you like it or not. Many who have been with him once refuse any second invitation he may make.'

Again Jeanette was filled with uneasiness. One moment she would tell herself that it must be all right, otherwise her two friends wouldn't be going; and the next moment Craig's warning would intrude, shutting out all else. She had absolutely no knowledge of rock climbing and, recalling the various pictures she had seen of men on an almost vertical rock face, her heart seemed to turn a somersault. It left her feeling quite sick and as she journeyed home, sitting beside Çetin, she felt ready to abandon the whole idea, even at this late stage.

'Don't forget,' he said brusquely as he dropped her off at the steps leading to the front door. 'A very early night tomorrow. I don't want anyone falling behind with fatigue. It's hard going and you'll need a reserve of energy.'

Jeanette stood by the car, hesitantly, but before she could find the courage to disclose her fears Çetin had let in the clutch and, with an abrupt lift of his hand, he swung the car round and drove away.

There was still time, of course, she thought as she made to enter the house. If her courage still failed her she could always send a message.

'Jeanette ... over here!' Her brother's voice reached her from the patio and she went round the side of the house to where the coloured lights hung from the trees. She was glad Mark was at home, for she hadn't yet mentioned the trip to him. She had had the odd conviction that he would worry, and had decided not to tell him anything about it, allowing him to think she was spending another week-end with Gwen and Sally. But now she felt guilty, for it seemed faintly deceitful not to inform him that she was going on Çetin's climbing expedition. To her consternation Craig was there, leaning back in a wicker chair, a glass of vodka on the table at his elbow. 'You didn't tell me you were going over to Büyük Ada with Craig tomorrow evening.' Mark looked inquiringly at her, while picking up a bottle to pour her a drink. 'He's been waiting hours to see you.'

For a moment she could not look at Craig. Had he heard her and Çetin talking? He must have done; in any case, he couldn't possibly have missed hearing the car. He made no comment on what her brother had been saying, but spoke softly, asking who had brought her home. He already knew, she thought, her heart fluttering at the cold dark fury in his eyes. She could not answer him. What right had he to assume that expression? Why did he make her feel like this – half afraid of him, and guilty? She swallowed painfully, releasing that little grip of fear, but for some quite incomprehensible reason her eyelids pricked and her lashes were suddenly damp. She spoke quietly, amazing herself by the calmness of her tone.

'I'm not coming, Craig. We didn't make any definite arrangement for this week-end, and I'm going somewhere else.' Even as she spoke her spirits sank lower. This settled her indecision; she would have to go with Çetin now otherwise it would appear that she had lied. Not only would Craig be puzzled by this, but Mark would be sure to ask the reason.

'You ...?' Craig seemed unable to frame his words. With a sudden shock of surprise she knew he would have had no such difficulty had Mark not been there. He would have assumed that same authoritative manner which had so surprised and angered her on the occasion of her illness, when he had taken it upon himself to send Çetin home. 'True, we didn't make a definite date, but I naturally concluded it would be this week-end – as Mother and Diane have now left.' He spoke softly, suppressing his anger because of Mark. 'Do you mind telling me where you're going?' he added, in no way put out by her brother's swift glance of surprise.

There was the slightest hesitation before Jeanette said, 'I'm going with Sally and Gwen – on a trip.'

'Trip?' It was Mark who spoke, and as Craig's eyes moved from his to Jeanette's she wondered, not without a tingling of apprehension, if Craig were making a guess at the truth. 'You never said anything to me about it. Where are you going?'

Craig picked up his glass and took a drink, watching Jeanette and awaiting the reply to her brother's question.

'We're going to Bursa—' She was interrupted by the telephone ringing in the house. Mark rose at once, before she herself could offer to answer it, and so make her escape.

'May I ask what you're going to Bursa for?' inquired Craig, returning his glass to the table with a slow, deliberate movement.

She looked up, pale but resolute. Craig's interest, as always, puzzled her, but now she was determined to end it once and for all.

'I don't want to offend you, Craig,' she said quietly, 'but what I do is my own affair. Several times you've thought fit to interfere, but please don't in future. I want—' To her dismay her voice trembled and began to break, and it was with difficulty that she finished what she had to say. 'I want to be left alone – to manage my own – my own life.'

A profound silence. A breeze fluttered in, catching up some heady perfume and spreading it across the garden. Craig spoke at last, his anger gone, replaced once again by that cold indifference which had characterized his attitude on first becoming acquainted with her several months ago.

'Certainly you must do as you please – I shall neither interfere nor advise again—' And then, as if he couldn't help himself, 'You did intend assisting me, Jeanette, but something has happened – something you refuse to bring out into the open.' Bitterness crept into his voice as he added, 'I wouldn't have expected you to go back on your word.' He shook his head as if still unable to accept it. 'No, not you.' He rose, moving his glass to the centre of the table. 'Say good night to Mark for me, will you?' And with that curt request he was gone. She stared after him, watching his long strides as he covered the distance down the garden, making for the narrow strip of shingle that fringed the waterfront. She understood his disappointment. He had aimed to finish the book by the end of the year. On his own admission he had not made a great deal of progress lately. Naturally he had hoped that her assistance would help him to finish the book on time – but she had let him down; let him down after making a sincere promise. No wonder he had regarded her with that icy stare of disbelief! Tears began to blur her vision and she left the patio and walked round to the front of the house. Mark was in the hall, still on the telephone; she whispered Craig's message and her own good night, then went upstairs, hoping for the solace and forgetfulness of sleep.

The three girls were enchanted with Bursa, for it was a beautiful city, built on the foothills of Ulüdağ and commanding a magnificent view across the wide and fertile Plain of Bursa. After the long car journey they would have been content to stay in the city, for there was so much of interest to see; beautiful mosques, the famous towel market and, to their surprise and delight, it proved to be an antique hunter's paradise.

'I want that copper tray,' Sally stated firmly, and would have proceeded to bargain for it had not Çetin caught her arm.

'Don't be ridiculous; we've come here to climb. You can't carry that thing about with you.'

'Must we climb?' put in Gwen, her eyes on a superb porcelain group. 'I'm quite content to potter around here.'

'So am I,' put in Jeanette hopefully, but the girls' words were greeted with stares of amazement by Çetin and his two friends.

'It seems crazy climbing a mountain when there's a perfectly good road one can drive along,' said Gwen, almost stooping under the weight of her pack.

'And why bring sleeping bags when there are such wonderful hotels?' Sally wanted to know as both she and Jeanette trudged along in the rear. Çetin turned, his lips compressed; clearly he had never taken out a party such as this. Noting his expression, the girls began to giggle. The Turks were so stolid, and so unswerving. If they set out to do something they did just that. The idea of abandoning one idea in favour of another – which, to the girls at least, promised to be much more exciting – would never have crossed Çetin's mind. He had come to climb, and that was what he intended doing.

Jeanette could never afterwards remember the route they took. She scarcely remembered the pine woods, the curious rock formation – but she did remember the icy water through which they had to wade, the scorpions, the terrifying thunder storm which drove them from their sleeping bags to the shelter of the rocks where debris came hurtling down, carried by the torrential rain which drenched them to the skin and caused their teeth to chatter with the cold. Yet through it all Çetin and the other two young Turks remained calmly unmoved. It was easy to see that to them these occurrences were all part of the trip, uncomfortable, perhaps, but not unduly disturbing. When the three girls had stood by the icy stream, hopefully believing that the project would have to be abandoned after all, Çetin had curtly told them to take off their jeans and wade across. He and his friends were already clad in high rubber leggings.

'Wade across in – What do you think we are, Çetin? You can put that idea right out of your mind!' Sally, usually so good-humoured, was at last beginning to lose patience with Çetin.

'Do you think we are going to look at you?' he rasped, his anger rising. 'We're here to *climb*, I've told you!' He meant that, the girls were quite convinced. To him the way he suggested was the obvious one, the most sensible. Nevertheless, the girls rolled up their jeans above their knees and, their boots in their hands, stepped gingerly into the water. When they reached the opposite side their legs were blue and their jeans were dripping wet.

Later, the three girls had a little conference to decide whether or not to leave Çetin and his companions to carry on alone.

'But how will we get back?' asked Gwen doubtfully.

'I expect we could hire a car. The tourists obviously do.'

'Is it worth the trouble?'

'We're going to look pretty foolish if we turn back now.'

'I hadn't thought of that.'

'No ... we would look foolish,' Jeanette agreed, for all their friends and acquaintances knew of the trip. And one or two, aware of Çetin's reputation, had grinned, saying they hoped they wouldn't regret it. 'Perhaps we've got over the worst.' They were sitting in a clearing, having a snack, and the way ahead did not seem too bad at all. Wooded slopes, with no sign of any sheer rock faces.

'Yes – oh, let's go on,' said Gwen. 'After all, it does add to one's prestige to say one has climbing among one's accomplishments.'

Jeanette's optimism as to the worst of their troubles being over soon proved a forlorn hope. After Çetin had decided on a clearing on the mountainside as their resting-place, and told them to get out their sleeping bags, Gwen suddenly jumped high into the air and screamed,

'Scorpions! We can't sleep here, Çetin!'

Looking swiftly down, Jeanette and Sally both moved, but the scorpions were all around them.

'Don't mind them,' said Çetin calmly as he and Ali began to tread the scorpions down with their heavy boots. 'Come on, clear a place. Don't stand there!'

There was nothing for it but to do as they were told.

'Oh, well,' said Sally with a shrug of resignation, 'it's adventure – and I expect we'll have a laugh about it later on.'

The storm began at midnight, and raged for hours; they all stood huddled into the tiny space under the cliff which rose starkly above them. But the next morning the sun shone brilliantly, gleaming on the snow-capped summit of Ulüdağ. Everyone's spirits rose, as, packing up, they continued their ascent of the mountain.

It was only a couple of hours later when, roped together, they were tackling the rock face. To her surprise Jeanette was thoroughly enjoying it. Being sensible enough not to look down, she experienced no fear at all. The mountain air was cold and invigorating, and Jeanette began to feel the pride of achievement as, now and then, Çetin would throw them a word of encouragement or, more grudgingly, a word of praise.

Then suddenly someone shouted, 'rocks!' and always afterwards Jeanette remembered her reaction. What did it mean? There were rocks all around. In any case, she had not connected the shout with her own safety. This reaction must have been experienced in a flash, however, for the next moment, with a second cry echoing in her ears, she felt the searing pain in her thigh, was conscious of its being ripped open, of blood everywhere – and that she had released her precarious hold on the narrow protruding ledge. . . .

CHAPTER SIX

HER eyes fluttered open and Mark was there; Mark, looking pale and drawn and very tired. Jeanette closed her eyes again; her leg was twice its size and throbbing with pain.

'I remember it,' she murmured. 'They couldn't get me down. . . .' She shuddered. 'I wanted to go down – but they brought me up.'

'Çetin thought it would be easier.' Her brother's voice came soothingly, and as if from a distance: 'You're in the hotel.'

'I did want to go down. . . .' She remembered her terror at the idea of going up. Down seemed *safe*. It was the solid ground beneath her feet and she had implored them to take her down. 'I'm such a long way up.'

'But quite safe, dear. We shall take you down soon, by road.'

'I wanted to go down—' Her hands clenched till the knuckles shone white beneath the skin. 'Why didn't they take me down?' She looked at him, a dazed expression on her face.

'It would have been too difficult, dear,' Mark answered patiently. 'You're going down very soon, very slowly and safely, in the car.'

She opened her eyes wide, and saw again how drawn he looked. Something else there too; such deep anxiety worried her.

'Am I very ill?' she asked, and instantly he shook his head.

'It's only the leg. That's bad – very bad, but the doctor says it won't take too long to heal. You've had several stitches—'

'Have I? I didn't know.' Vaguely she remembered an injection, and the blessed release from pain. 'I'd be conscious when they did it.' She paused, again wondering at the trouble in his eyes. 'What is it, Mark? Is something worrying you?'

He smiled then, and shook his head, but Jeanette knew instinctively that he was only trying to reassure her.

'Nothing is worrying me – and *you* mustn't worry about a thing, either. Would you like to close your eyes and rest again now?'

'I'm not tired. When are we going home?' and before he could reply, 'Where are the others?'

'They've already gone – all except Sally. She insisted on staying; she'll come down with us.'

'That was good of her.'

'I'm going to phone the doctor now,' he told her. 'He did say there would be no difficulty – that you could be moved tonight, but he also said he'd like to see you first.'

'What time is it?'

'Almost five o'clock.'

'Still Sunday?'

'Still Sunday.' He smiled, smoothed the bed cover, and left her. A moment or two later Sally came in and sat on the side of the bed; she too looked troubled, but at the same time relieved.

'So you've come round. How do you feel?'

'Fine, if my leg didn't hurt so much. How did you manage to get Mark here so soon?'

'We phoned him right away, and by some miracle there was a plane from Istanbul and he managed to get it. He was here in no time at all.'

'He didn't come by car? How are we to get home?'

'Mark's hired a car, an outsize one. It's been waiting quite a while. We'll be going soon; the doctor didn't foresee any hitch at all.'

'Sally. . . .' Jeanette hesitated and then, 'Sally, is there anything else wrong? I mean, Mark seems so very troubled about something.'

'Troubled?' Sally looked rather blank. 'I expect he's dreadfully worried about you, naturally.'

'It isn't that.' She moved her head against the pillow, a frown upon her brow. 'I know it's silly, but he looks – sort of – shattered.'

A frown touched her friend's brow at that.

'I don't understand. You're probably imagining things, being as you are.'

'You mean I'm not quite myself?' Jeanette said, smiling faintly.

'Well, you have been drugged, you know. And you were rambling – I didn't hear you because the doctor sent us all away, but Mark said you were rambling. He seemed somewhat put out by the things you said,' she added, her frown deepening slightly in sudden recollection. 'Yes, now I come to think of it, he did seem rather shaken as he was telling me.'

'Telling you?' She looked at her friend curiously, lifting her head from the pillow. 'What was I saying?'

'Oh, he didn't tell me that – just said you were rambling.'

'And he seemed . . . shaken . . .?' What could she have said to affect Mark in that way? What else had been in Mark's expression? What else besides anxiety? She tried to think, to see his face again— Pity, compassion, yes, those had been there . . .! She shook her head in bewilderment, then laid it back against the pillow. 'I wonder what I said. I must ask him.'

The doctor having announced her fit to be moved, Jeanette was carried to the car and settled comfortably along the back seat, with her friend on the seat opposite. Mark sat in the front with the driver who went slowly and with extreme care along the mountain road. It was very late when they arrived in Istanbul. They dropped Sally first; Jeanette thanked her and so did Mark. Sally brushed off their thanks and said she'd be over to see Jeanette the following day after school.

Jeanette was put straight to bed, Tony stayed with her and Mark for a while and then left them alone. The silence seemed strange and after having a little difficulty in framing her question, Jeanette asked her brother what she had said when under the influence of the drug. He glanced up, startled for a moment, and then his eyes softened and assumed that compassionate expression of which she had been vaguely aware of a few hours earlier.

'It was very much of a jumble,' he replied non-committally. 'You were just rambling, Jeanette ... it didn't make very much sense.' And then, getting up from the chair, 'I'm turning in now. Don't forget to ring the bell if you want anything. Mrs. Baydur has been told to come up at once. Good night, Jeanette.'

'Good night, Mark.' She watched him go to the door. 'Mark. . . .'

'Yes?' He turned, his hand on the edge of the open door.

'Does – does Craig know about this?' She spoke with difficulty, aware of her heightened colour, but more profoundly aware of the sudden movement in her brother's throat ... almost as if he were trying to swallow a hard little lump there.

'He went to the *yali*, as you know. I left a note; he would get it on his return.' He paused and went on with seeming reluctance. 'I thought he might have called – or phoned.'

'And he hasn't.' The words came out against her will; her brother spoke with an odd urgency, telling her that he might not yet be home.

'He sometimes does leave it until Monday – even Tuesday, as you know.'

'Yes.' Her eyes pricked suddenly. 'You remember he wanted me to help him with his book?' And, when he nodded, 'If I'd gone to Büyük Ada this wouldn't have happened.'

A tightness touched the corners of his mouth.

'It wouldn't,' he agreed, 'but on the other hand—'

'Well?' She waited a while for him to continue. 'What were you going to say?'

'Nothing, nothing important.' He bade her good night

84

once more and went out, closing the door softly behind him.

For the next fortnight Jeanette had to stay in bed, but the gash in her thigh was healing rapidly and without any sign of complication.

'You'll carry a scar, I'm afraid,' the doctor told her, 'but you're very lucky not to be left with anything worse. Climbing's all very well for those who have studied the technique, but damned silly for a novice like you.' The doctor was a tall and slender Turk who had a permanent scowl and thick black eyebrows that met over his nose giving him a most ferocious appearance. He spoke English better than many an Englishman, for he studied languages, and it was said that he spoke over twenty. Jeanette was rather scared of him, expecting him any day to pronounce the need for the 'evil spirit' to be released. This would mean a quick incision, probably on her brow, and as Jeanette had heard many accounts of this attack with a scalpel – for he permitted no resistance – she always viewed his departing figure with the utmost relief.

'I don't think you need worry,' Gwen said, trying to reassure her. 'It's the village folk, mainly – they expect it. Wouldn't think they were cured unless the evil spirit was allowed to escape.'

'But he cut Sally's head, didn't he?'

'Yes, he did,' Gwen owned. 'We'd only been here a couple of weeks when she contracted jaundice, and he insisted that she have the evil blood released. Don't know what the difference is, but apparently if you have one thing wrong with you it's the evil spirit that must be cast out, and with some other ailment it's the blood. Terribly superstitious these people are – they seem to be like this in all these eastern countries.'

'Sally tells me you're both going home for the summer holiday,' Jeanette said, changing the subject. 'I shall miss you terribly.'

'It's our mums – you know what they are; always

worrying because we're so far from the safety of their loving care. In their day girls didn't go running off all over the place; there wasn't the same chance, I suppose. But although they accept our being away they don't like it. Sally's mum's worse than mine because of course she's an only one.' She paused as Jeanette moved, finding a cooler place for her leg under the thin linen bed cover. 'All right?'

Jeanette smiled faintly and nodded, going on to say she wished she was back at school.

'It's so miserable here all day on my own. Still, I suppose I should be thankful that I'm no worse.'

'Yes, indeed.' Gwen's face paled slightly at the recollection of those terrible few moments when the great rocks came hurtling down the mountainside. 'I'll never forget it as long as I live. I thought you were going to be killed.'

'I didn't actually see them. I think I must be a complete idiot, for I didn't even think of getting out of the way. I had no idea what they meant when they shouted the warning.'

'It was Çetin's fault. Apparently that's his main trouble; he takes it for granted that you know – and also that you know how to act in these sort of situations. An experienced climber would have easily avoided the accident.'

'So would I, had I thought; because it was only my leg. Had I moved only slightly to one side I'd have escaped any injury at all.' Again she changed the subject, depressed by the prospect of her friends' departure for England and wondering what she would do with herself during the long summer vacation. 'Are you spending the whole nine weeks away?'

Gwen nodded, reluctantly.

'We're travelling by car, so that's going to cut out a week at either end of the holiday. We could do it quicker, I know, but we want to see a few places on the way. We have to take the car in order to bring back all the things you can't buy here. If there's anything you want you must tell us.'

'I find it's clothes, mainly, they're not very nice here, and you can't buy those for me.' Not that she would need many clothes, she mused, still unable to throw off her dejection at the idea of being without Sally and Gwen for so long at a time. Her sun-suit would suffice, for she could see herself spending the whole of the vacation sitting in the garden with a book.

'No . . . well, if you do think of anything, make a list; it's only three weeks; we break up at the end of June, you know.'

Gwen had not been gone many minutes when Mark came in, a couple of books under his arm. He looked tired and pushed a hand through his dark wavy hair.

'Have you a headache?' she asked anxiously as he threw down the books on the bed.

'It's that blasted *odos* again. It blew up from Marmara so strongly today that it stopped the car ferries, and it's so hot. The air's leaden, and everyone seems so irritable – I suppose I'm lucky, it's given me the most damnable headache, but that's all.' He glanced at her critically. 'Are *you* all right?'

'Yes, it doesn't seem to have affected me this time.'

'Good. It's dying down now.' He picked up one of the books again, handing it to her, saying, without much expression,

'Craig's sent these. This one's a sort of guide book, describing the treasures of Topkapi, and the other is the history of the Ottoman Turks. He said he'd promised, some time ago, to lend it to you.'

'Yes, he did.' Jeanette swallowed hard. 'Thank him for me, won't you, Mark?'

'He's coming over tomorrow, when you're up, so you can thank him yourself.' He looked straight at her, then away again, and she hoped he hadn't noticed how the colour tinged her cheeks or her fingers trembled as she took the guide book from his outstretched hand. Craig had called twice only, during the past fortnight; on both occasions his manner was cool and remote, reminding her again of that first month when he had seemed so determined to keep her at a distance. His first visit was on the Monday, immediately after his arrival from Büyük Ada. Jeanette had steeled herself, expecting to see censure in his eyes and be subjected to a cutting reproof for not heeding his warning. This, she discovered with a slight sense of shock, would have been far preferable to the stiff, impersonal inquiries which sounded perfunctory and devoid of any real concern.

The following week-end he had gone again to the island, remaining until Tuesday, but this week-end he was obviously staying at home. He came after lunch on Sunday; Jeanette, sitting in the garden, her leg still swollen and heavily bandaged, saw him in the distance, striding along the narrow waterfront, intent on the busy traffic – vessels of all shapes and sizes, plying through the waters of the Bosphorus, north to the Black Sea and south to the placid, sub-tropical waters of Marmara.

He entered through the small gate at the end of the garden, seeming to walk more slowly now, yet covering the distance rapidly with his long and easy strides.

Reaching her, he stood looking down, his dark face proud and set, his shoulders erect. But he had a rather drawn expression, and lines around his eyes. She wondered if he had been working too hard; or perhaps he hadn't slept, thinking of Diane. He must be missing her terribly, Jeanette thought.

His eyes flickered, noting the bulge in her dress caused by the swelling in her thigh and by the protecting wad of cotton wool beneath the bandages.

So confident and self-possessed he looked, despite the tiredness round his eyes. She wondered if there'd ever been an occasion in his life when he'd lacked this cool composure as, awkwardly, she indicated a nearby chair, inviting him to sit down. She glanced back, wondering what her brother and Tony were doing and hoping fervently that they had not become engrossed in anything which would keep them too long indoors.

'Thank you for the books, Craig.'

'That's all right. There are plenty more there if you want them.'

'Thank you,' she said again, looking down at her hands in her lap; then she lifted her eyes again to glance beyond him to the ships passing through the strait.

'You look much better than when I last saw you. Mark informs me that the wound is healing quickly now.'

'Yes – I didn't walk downstairs, but I did walk about inside. I haven't any pain at all now.' Such a flat uninteresting conversation. Jeanette looked round again. What had happened to Mark and Tony? They had said they were following her out, in a moment or two. She returned her attention to the water traffic.

'They're here,' said Craig sardonically, reading her thoughts. She blushed hotly; he did not spare her. 'Perhaps you'll now relax.'

'I'm sorry—' Mark sat down, looking anxiously at Jeanette. She stared. She had the most curious impression that he was apologizing for leaving her alone with Craig!

Tony came up and to Jeanette's dismay he mentioned the accident and the conversation became centred on that for the next ten minutes or so.

'Çetin should have given them some drill,' Mark asserted after Tony had said some disparaging things about the young Turk. 'It's absolutely stupid to take inexperienced people up a mountain without advising them how to act in the face of possible danger.'

'It was just unfortunate,' submitted Jeanette, avoiding Craig's eyes. 'It isn't quite fair to blame Çetin.'

'Çetin is to blame! He's an expert climber and knows the hazards. Why he wants to take people like you I don't know!' Craig spoke harshly, all his dislike of Çetin revealed in his tone. Jeanette said nothing; she still avoided his gaze.

'That wasn't all, from what Sally and Gwen told me,' said Mark, turning to Jeanette. 'I believe you were soaked to the skin crossing some river—'

'No, it was only a stream,' Jeanette put in quickly.

'But you did get soaked?'

She had to admit that they did, whereupon Craig wanted to know how they had dried their clothes.

'It was only our jeans,' she said faintly. 'They – they dried on us.'

'They—!' Craig's lips compressed, but whatever else he had in mind was left unsaid, for Mark was now relating the incident of the scorpions.

But it wasn't the scorpions that interested Craig.

'Jeanette,' he said in tones of utter disbelief, and apparently forgetting the presence of the other two, 'do you mean to say you slept in the open?' Into his voice had crept that authority, that disciplinary inflection which had so angered her on the night he had sent Çetin away, and Jeanette's eyes flickered in bewilderment. He had said he would never interfere again, but it seemed that he had completely forgotten that previous assertion, for he was certainly interfering now. But why should he? Why should he care what she did or where she went? 'You actually slept in the open ... three men and three girls?'

'Oh, I say, Craig—' Mark broke off, his eyes remaining fixed on Craig in puzzlement. He, like Jeanette, seemed baffled by his friend's attitude.

Forcing herself to meet his gaze, Jeanette searched Craig's face, afraid of what she would see there. His opinion was of no consequence, she told herself ... and yet she felt she couldn't bear it if his eyes held cold contempt, disgust. What she did see made her gasp and suddenly recall his wrathful comment about doing her an injury.

He certainly looked as if he could do her an injury now!

He was awaiting a reply, too, but although Jeanette had difficulty in speaking she was surprised to find that her embarrassment was due to the presence of Tony and Mark, rather than to that of Craig himself.

At last she began to explain, saying they hadn't really slept owing to the storm, but at the same time endeavouring to skip lightly over their discomfiture. Noting the outraged expressions that her narrative brought forth she dismally concluded that she'd failed, and it certainly didn't help when Tony exclaimed,

'And your clothes again dried on you!'

'The sun came up . . . it didn't take long.'

'Really, Jeanette. . . .' It was Mark who now regarded her in disbelief, and for the first time his dark eyes held stern censure. 'The three of you appear to have shown an amazing lack of common sense. Why, in heaven's name, didn't you come home?'

'At midnight? We couldn't have found our way down.'

'It seems to me that you'd had plenty of warnings long before then,' Craig began wrathfully when she interrupted him.

'Please. . . .' Her glance embraced them all. 'Can we change the subject?' Her plea succeeded, but as the conversation drifted into other channels Craig remained silent, his lips tightly compressed. Why was he so furiously angry? Jeanette pondered over this for some time and then, suddenly, the explanation became quite clear. It was the book again. She could understand just how he felt – that she would have been far better occupied at the *yali* helping him than undergoing these unnecessary hazards.

He did relax, however, as the afternoon wore on, and even accepted Mark's invitation to stay to afternoon tea, which they had in a little arbour, under the shade of the Judas trees. And it was while they were having tea that Jeanette learned of the holiday planned by Tony and Mark. They were going to Lake Van in eastern Turkey, along with two other lecturers from the university. The round trip would be about two thousand miles and they would be away for six or seven weeks.

'You'll be all right,' said Mark, unconcernedly. 'I expect you've arranged something with Sally and Gwen?'

She glanced up quickly, about to tell him that her friends were going home, but she refrained. Mark would not hesitate to forfeit his holiday if he thought she was going to be alone.

'There'll be something to do,' she returned lightly, and then, 'I believe Lake Van's marvellous. Sally and Gwen went there, soon after they came over.'

'Yes, it is a wonderful place,' agreed Tony. 'The other two have already been, but Mark and I are quite looking forward to our first visit.' He turned to Craig. 'Are you going anywhere special?'

'I shall be at the *yali* for most of the time, but I had thought of a flying visit to England, just to see one or two friends.'

One or two friends . . . and Diane.

Jeanette now regarded with dismay the long holiday to which she had so eagerly looked forward. It had never dawned on her that her friends would go home, and she had contemplated a round of sightseeing, with Asiatic Turkey as the main objective. There was so much to see over there, especially the archaeological sites which, unlike those of Greece, had scarcely been explored. Gwen and Sally had told her about one they set out to find. The vicinity was known, but the actual site was grown over and no one had bothered very much about it. To the girls' delight they found it, and after Jeanette had been shown the exciting slides she had vaguely imagined that some similar exploration would form part of her holiday activities.

All this would take her mind off Craig – perhaps she'd be completely cured by the end of the vacation. But now it seemed that she would be quite alone, and for the first time since she had come out to Turkey Jeanette experienced that old feeling of loneliness and despair. She tried to think of Ned, but his image still eluded her. 'Time will heal, despite your present conviction to the contrary,' her mother had said, and it was so. But what of this other ache that had come so quickly to take its place?

Suddenly, for no apparent reason, she recalled that Craig had promised to take her over to the Asiatic side, had enthused about the beauties to be found there, quaint villages and ruined castles, and that lovely stretch of country ... the Sweet Waters of Asia, where the ladies of the aristocracy, yashmaked and bejewelled, had once drifted idly along in their gilded barges.

She wondered if her unhappiness showed on her face, for quite abruptly Craig looked across at her and said,

'You're tired, Jeanette. I should go to bed if I were you.' His tone was cool, impersonal, but his eyes seemed to hold a hint of concern and a smile fluttered as she rose, agreeing that she did feel tired and saying she would take his advice and lie down, though on the couch in the sitting-room.

'I don't feel like going to bed yet,' she added, still smiling up at him. 'I've had enough of that bedroom for a while.'

'Of course,' he agreed, on a surprisingly sympathetic note. 'Can you walk all right, or shall I help you?' He had already risen, but she cast a quick imploring glance at her brother. Far too disturbing to feel Craig's arm on hers.

He noticed her glance; his hand dropped to his side and his eyes glinted, cold as steel.

'Ah ... you'd better sit down again,' said Mark. 'Here come your friends.' They all turned as the car drew to a standstill in the drive and Sally and Gwen appeared. They knew she would be up on Sunday and had said they might call, although no specific time had been stated. Gwen carried a large spray of flowers which she immediately presented to Jeanette.

'Çetin sends his love and says will it be all right if he calls tomorrow evening? He would have come sooner, but he's been on duty non-stop for a fortnight.'

93

'They're beautiful. ...' Bending her head, Jeanette enjoyed their perfume for a moment, thinking there was no gift quite like flowers. ... Suddenly her thoughts defied her stern control – the control she had successfully kept upon them for the whole of the afternoon. Before she could prevent herself, she had raised her head to look at Craig. If only it were he. ...

She encountered a look of icy contempt, heard his voice saying stiffly that it was time he was going. She saw him stride away, his shoulders square and set; and then she heard Gwen mention her name, and was drawn into the conversation going on around her.

CHAPTER SEVEN

ÇETIN was full of apologies for the accident, admitting that the blame was mostly his. Although agreeing with her brother that Çetin should have given them all some idea of what might happen, Jeanette was so impressed with his obvious sincerity that she took the blame on herself, saying she had been very stupid not to realize at once that the cry was in fact an urgent warning.

'In any case, it doesn't matter now,' she said with a smile. 'I'm very much improved and the doctor says that in a couple of weeks I'll be able to walk about the house and the garden as much as I like.'

'I don't suppose you'll ever come with me again.' His voice held a distinct note of regret which puzzled her. He would persuade others to join him, she felt sure, having heard of his success in arousing people's enthusiasm for climbing.

'I'm afraid my brother would be very much against it,' she had to admit. 'He does feel responsible for me while I'm out here, which is only natural.' She could have added that her experience had in any case cured her of climbing for life, but she refrained.

'And your friend, Craig Fleming?' His voice rasped; the dislike was mutual, obviously. 'What had he to say about it?'

Removing a cushion, Jeanette leant back on the settee, her eyes on the little perfume jar, her mind going back to that evening when Craig had so admired it, telling her, with such confidence, of its great age. She thought with a sudden tightness in her throat that it would always remind her of Craig, and ever in the future she would see those strong brown hands holding it with that gentleness, that almost loving care.

'My activities are not his concern,' was her quiet reply,

her eyes still on the primitive clay jar, and her mind giving back those hours at Topkapi with Craig. They had been a pleasant and happy interlude then ... they were a very precious memory now.

'You're quite right, your activities are not his concern,' came the grim rejoinder, 'but he thinks fit to interfere. You haven't answered my question, Jeanette.'

'He wasn't pleased, Çetin, I must be honest. But as I've said, it doesn't matter now. You mustn't worry about it, or blame yourself. It's all over, and best forgotten.'

'Did he know you were coming?'

'I can't say; he may have done. If so, he guessed, because I didn't mention that we were going to climb.'

'I didn't think you had, otherwise you wouldn't have been able to come.' He sounded sulky, she thought, and wondered why. He had never tried to carry their relationship beyond the stage of friendship, so he couldn't be in any way jealous of Craig. 'He'd have done something to stop you.'

'He could hardly prevent me from doing anything I wanted to do,' she returned, recalling that, not so long ago, the very idea of Craig's interference had filled her with anger, and wondering why a similar reaction was not experienced now. Had Craig known what she was contemplating? She recollected her suspicions that he'd made a guess. Well, if he had, he'd made no attempt to prevent her from going, and that, she concluded, was the result of her own emphatic assertion that she wished for no further interference in her affairs.

'He stopped you coming out once,' he reminded her, and a flush leapt to her cheeks.

'On that occasion his action was justified, as it happened. I was badly affected by the *odos,* as you know. I didn't realize what was wrong, merely thinking it was tiredness, which would pass, but Craig recognized the symptoms and advised me not to go out.'

'Advised?' Çetin's dark brows lifted. 'He *made* you stay in, and I was damned annoyed about it.'

96

'Really, Çetin, it scarcely matters now,' she said with slight impatience. 'Don't look so vexed.'

He smiled faintly then, and for the first time Jeanette felt disturbed by his gaze. His next words disturbed her even more, shocked her in fact as, moving closer to her on the couch, he said, a litttle hoarsely,

'Did Sally give you my love?'

'Yes.' She glanced up, startled. 'But I—'

'I meant it, Jeanette – oh, I know this is sudden, but it was only when I held you on those rocks, when you clung to me, imploring me to take you down and looking at me, so scared, with those lovely eyes— Until that moment you'd meant nothing; you were just another English girl – we've had dozens here at the school, for they don't stay long. But you're so beautiful—'

'Çetin – please—' She raised a protesting hand, trying to continue, but he would not let her.

'I have never felt like that – oh, there have been a few Turkish girls, but they meant nothing. If only you knew how I felt, how your fear of being taken up touched me—' He broke off, his face suddenly grim. 'I almost did take you down – me, who knows the best way! I almost took a chance – which would have been madness – all because of your pleading. I wanted to do only what you wished, Jeanette, and it will always be that way.'

'No ... oh, Çetin. ...' She was hot and embarrassed, but at the same time regretful that he should be hurt. Vaguely, she recalled Craig's intense dislike of this man, and began to doubt if there were any real basis for it, because there was no doubt at all about Çetin's sincerity; she knew he spoke the truth when he asserted that she was the first girl who had mattered, and that his one desire was to please her.

How could she explain? She turned, noticing the anxiety in his eyes where previously there had been indifference, the strange humility which replaced his natural pride.

She shook her head, unable to find words that would

not be too hurtful. She thought of her own love for Craig and her sympathy grew.

'Everything is wrong,' she murmured, almost to herself. 'Everything is upside down.'

'What . . .?' He seemed a little dazed, uncertain – and this was so unlike him. 'You cannot care for me?'

That should have made it easy, but the hurt in his eyes and his voice brought a lump to her throat. Again she shook her head, sadly.

'No, Çetin, I'm sorry. . . .'

'I have been too sudden – not tactful and – and patient. Is that it? English girls – what sort of an approach do they want?' He was pleading; she had never had a harder task in her life than telling him, firmly, that she could never love him.

'You don't want to marry me because I'm Turkish—'

'That isn't it at all,' she swiftly denied. 'That wouldn't make any difference – why should it – if I cared?'

'You like the Turks?' He appeared heartened, and hopeful.

'Of course I do. I would never stay in a country if I didn't like the people.' Certainly there was a dourness about the Turks, but only on the surface. Underneath it they were a friendly, generous race; a little too conventional perhaps, but who could say whether or not that was a fault? In any case, it was unimportant.

'Then—' He put out a hand, as if to take her hers, but changed his mind. 'I believe, as I have said, that this is too sudden, too much of a surprise. Promise me, Jeanette, that you will think about it.'

Already she was shaking her head, and at last Çetin appeared to accept his fate. But he did go on to ask Jeanette to go out with him on occasions. She had never yet done so, not without the company of others. The only times she had been alone with him were on those occasions when he had brought her home in his car from some party or other entertainment.

'I don't know, Çetin, if it would be wise,' she said with

honesty. 'Not with your feeling like this.'

'You think I would harm you?'

'Certainly not, but—' She broke off, shrugging. It was so difficult to put her thoughts and doubts into words.

There was a little silence before Çetin spoke again and then, with a caution that faintly amused her, while at the same time arousing all her compassion,

'Sally and Gwen are going home, to England, for the holidays, so you will not have them. Will you let me take you around, and show you some of my country?'

Her instinct, naturally, was to refuse, but even as she hesitated he went on to make a solemn promise not to mention his feelings for her, never to embarrass her in any way. His sincerity seemed apparent, and as he continued, in what she had to admit was a very plausible manner, she felt that no harm could come from their going on a few outings together. Plainly Çetin would derive pleasure from her acceptance of his offer, and for herself ... it would at least ensure that she had one or two diversions in what threatened to be a lonely and monotonous summer vacation.

'Very well, Çetin,' she smiled. 'I'll let you take me around.'

During the next couple of weeks the wound healed rapidly, and at last the bandages were completely removed. Sometimes Jeanette would feel an ache, which caused her to limp slightly, but the doctor assured her that this aching would cease altogether in about a couple of months and in consequence the limp would disappear too. Everyone agreed that she had been lucky, and although Jeanette at first felt very conscious of the scar, when wearing her shorts or sun-suit, she felt a profound gratitude that no more serious injury had been sustained.

The evening before her friends' departure for England Jeanette went with them and several other young people to one of the fascinating little wooden cafés along the shores of the Bosphorus. There they sat eating *meze* and lobster and drinking *raki*. Later they went on to a night-club and watched the belly-dancers; it was long past midnight when they left and Çetin took Jeanette home.

'When are we going out?' he wanted to know as he drove right up to the front door.

'Ring me, Çetin,' she said, feeling too tired to think about arrangements for an outing. 'Mark and Tony will be going off the day after tomorrow, so get in touch with me after that.'

The following day she helped her brother and Tony with their preparations; they were going in Mark's car and as they expected difficulties with accommodation in the more out-of-the-way places, they were taking camping gear and cooking equipment. Jeanette had a tinge of guilt now and then when Mark, still quite unaware that she was staying at home all the time, would mention her own holiday, recommending some place or other, and telling her where to eat and what to see.

She couldn't think of telling Mark, for she was only too pleased that he had arranged this holiday. He worked so hard, putting everything into his job, and doing masses of preparation in the evenings.

But once they had gone she had the greatest difficulty in not indulging in a bout of self-pity; she felt so alone and lost. It was almost as if she had the place to herself for Mrs. Baydur and Metat kept to their own quarters in the annexe at the end of the house, and she saw them only at meal times.

Mark and Tony had been gone two days when Çetin rang; he had been on duty, much to his disappointment. He still had duties to do, but on his free days they went about, usually ending up at a night-club in the evenings. To Jeanette it was a futile round; she derived no pleasure from the visits to the places of interest, remembering always, those occasions when she had been out with Craig and recollecting that, at the time of the visit to Topkapi, she had been eagerly looking forward to further trips out with him. As for the evenings spent with Çetin, she felt that they must lead to something, for several times when he had brought her home she had sensed his desire to kiss her good night. After a week of sightseeing and night-clubs she began to wonder if she would be better to stay at home, reading her books and resting in the garden, and by the beginning of the second week she found herself searching for an excuse to refuse Çetin's next invitation.

During this time she had seen nothing of Craig, but, on talking to Murad, she learned that he was in England but would be back at the week-end. He wouldn't call, naturally, because Mark wasn't here; also he was, like her brother, under the impression that she was staying at the flat with Gwen and Sally, so there was no reason at all for his calling. However, Jeanette had reckoned without the chauffeur. Through Metat he discovered that she was still at home, and Murad passed on the information to Craig on his return. He called one afternoon; Jeanette was in the garden, sunbathing, her book beside her on the grass. Perhaps it was her imagination – because she was so sensitive about it – but Craig's eyes seemed instantly to flicker to the scar on her leg. But even as she made an instinctive movement to cover it with her hand, his gaze had already become fixed on her face.

'I'd no idea you were on your own here until Murad mentioned it.' Craig frowned at her and went on to ask why she had changed her mind about moving in with her friends for the summer. 'You told Mark that you intended doing so,' he went on, casting her a look of interrogation.

Jeanette shook her head.

'No, I didn't; he took it for granted and I merely refrained from telling him that Gwen and Sally had already arranged to spend the summer holiday in England.'

'They've gone to England?' And then, angrily, 'Why on earth didn't you tell Mark? He would never have allowed you to spend the summer all alone like this.' For a moment she wondered at his concern, but his next words provided an explanation. 'Has it occurred to you that he is going to feel very guilty about it when he discovers, on his return, that you've spent the entire vacation here on your own?'

She glanced up quickly.

'No, I didn't really think about it.' So his concern was for his friend's feelings, and not for her at all. 'I know he wouldn't have left me, and that's why I didn't tell him. Mark needs a holiday, Craig; he works so very hard.'

He said nothing for a moment, but his lips compressed. In spite of her explanation he was still annoyed with her for allowing her brother to remain in ignorance about her being alone.

'May I sit down?' he said, at the same time opening up a garden chair which lay folded on the grass.

'Of course – I'm sorry,' and then, awkwardly, 'Did you enjoy your holiday in England?'

'I had quite a pleasant time,' he returned non-committally. 'What are you doing with yourself?' He seemed anxious now and Jeanette found herself blushing. Before she could frame a reply he added tersely, 'Rustem?'

'He kindly offered to take me around.'

'I see.' A muscle moved at the corner of his mouth; his glance flicked with contempt. 'I should have thought you'd had enough of him for a while.'

'It's helped . . . going about with him.' The words were out before she could check them. They revealed so much, and she felt disloyal to Çetin, especially when Craig with his quick perception asked her bluntly if she were enjoying going about with the young Turk.

'I – that is—' She looked at him helplessly. No use saying she was enjoying herself because Craig had already guessed otherwise. She supposed he must have sensed her reluctance to tell him the truth, for he spoke to her in gentler tones, though not without a tiny spark of anger.

'You idiot, Jeanette. I'm sure you could have arranged things better than this.'

'I don't see how. I couldn't let Mark miss his holiday

just for me.'

'I can understand your anxiety,' he conceded, 'but I still think you could have arranged this differently. Couldn't you have gone to England with your friends?'

'I suppose I could, but when they first decided to go I didn't know that Mark would be away. Then Sally heard of a German couple who wanted a lift to Munich, so there wouldn't have been room in the car.' She looked up as Metat came out, to ask if she required anything. 'Would you like some coffee, Craig?' she asked, unaware of the plea in her voice, but fully aware of the pain she was giving herself by deliberately trying to prolong his visit.

'Thank you, Jeanette, I would.' Her eyes fluttered at the curious note in his voice as he added, after waiting for her to give instructions to Metat, 'We must do something about you,' and after a pause, 'We did say once that we'd go to Eyüp. Would you still like to do that? I'll willingly take you.'

Again he was thinking of his friend. If he took an interest in her, relieved the monotony by taking her about, then Mark would not be upset when, on his return, he discovered she had been without the company of her friends. Despite this conclusion as to the reason for Craig's offer, Jeanette's pulses quickened. To accept was madness. Inevitably she would suffer for her folly, would come bitterly to regret this abandon, this deliberate suppression of the warning which, even now, was clamouring to be heard.

But she must accept.

Nevertheless, a feeling of guilt came over her as she recalled that his original plan was to spend the time, after his return from England, on the island; and while reluctant to mention the book, seeing that she had let him down so badly over it, she felt she had to ask him why he wasn't intending to work on it.

'Aren't you going to Büyük Ada?' she added, and he merely replied, casually,

'I may go later; we'll see.'

She really ought to tell him she would be all right, and that he must go to the island and continue with his book, but for two reasons she refrained.

Firstly, knowing him so well. she suspected that, having made his decision, he would at once assume his coercive, arbitrary manner immediately any opposition or argument was put forward by her. Secondly, the prospect of being with Craig was too attractive, too alluring. Madness it might be, but she accepted his offer, at the same time thanking him for making it.

'I once said you mustn't thank me,' he reminded her gravely. 'I shall enjoy taking you out, Jeanette. I'm quite sure of that.'

Of course. . . . He, too, was on his own and probably welcomed the idea of having company. He must be very lonely, separated as he was from the woman he loved and wondering how long he would have to wait until she came to him.

Metat brought out the coffee; they began to drink it in companionable silence, but after a while Jeanette ventured to mention Çetin.

'What can I say to him?' She looked anxiously at Craig, who turned a steely gaze upon her.

'Are you committed in any way?'

'I did promise to let him take me out,' Jeanette murmured, averting her head.

A brief, tense silence followed.

'I take it you weren't enjoying his company overmuch?' She did not reply to that.

'I think you misjudge him, Craig,' was all she said.

Again that metallic gaze. She began to regret having mentioned Çetin. After all, there had been no need to do so; she could have told him she didn't want to go out with him again and that would have ended the matter. Craig need not have known anything about it.

'Supposing I hadn't come along,' said Craig, eyeing her searchingly, 'would you have continued to go around with him?'

She shook her head.

'I'd practically decided to stay at home—' She smiled rather bleakly. 'I could have caught up with my reading.'

'In that case, you have only to do what you intended. Tell him you don't want to go out with him again.' He dismissed Çetin; the conversation became more casual and once again there entered into their relationship that friendliness, that deep intimacy which Jeanette had always found so disturbing. Gone altogether was the restraint, the animosity that had been present on so many occasions when they were together. This promised well for the holiday, and although she heard again that warning, she ignored it.

The present was all that mattered. The future could take care of itself. Heartache it would assuredly bring ... but why forgo the preceding pleasure?

'Will you have some more coffee?' It did not occur to her, as she once more endeavoured to keep him, that he would guess at her intention, but as she noticed the quick change in his expression she would have done anything to take back the impulsive question.

'Look, Jeanette, why not come over to my place for dinner this evening? There doesn't seem to be much sense in each of us dining alone.'

'Oh, no, Craig! You mustn't put yourself out.'

'I am not,' he said, stressing his words, 'putting myself out.'

Was it pity? she wondered, her chin lifting as she rebelled against the idea.

'If you're feeling sorry for me—' she began, then stopped even before he interrupted, surprising her – as once before he had surprised her on a similar occasion – by saying, roughly, and with a distinct flare to his nostrils,

'One of these days, my girl, *you're* going to be sorry – sorry for yourself!' And, when her only reaction was to blush, and to look at him wide-eyed, her lips faintly parted, 'I'll expect you about seven.' As he rose to go his eyes once again sought the scar on her thigh. 'That should be covered; too much sun will do more harm than good. He stood looking down at her, a quizzical smile suddenly hovering on his lips. 'I expect that now I've suggested you keep it covered, you'll promptly make a firm resolution to leave it exposed.'

She laughed then, and Craig responded.

'As a matter of fact, you're wrong. I shall heed your suggestion.'

His brow came up quickly in well-feigned surprise.

'We're progressing,' was his faintly mocking rejoinder before, with a little salutatory lift of his hand, he turned abruptly and strode away.

The first hint of twilight had entered the sky when Jeanette arrived at Craig's house. She had on a plain cotton dress in a delicate shade of green, short-sleeved and trimmed with a white lace collar and cuffs which contrasted charmingly with her deeply tanned skin. Over her arm she carried a wrap, just in case the breeze came up later, when she was returning home.

Craig, immaculate in beige linen, was on the steps of the patio, waiting for her. She stopped, lifting her head to smile. She was happy, living in the present, and with no desire to dwell either on the past or the future. Her happiness was reflected in her smile, and the faint flush that rose to her cheeks. All around the air was heady, and so still. Stars were vaguely present in the changing light, while down below the fishermen's lanterns sprang up one by one to cast their reflections into the darkening waters of the Bosphorus. Craig's gaze was inexpressive; no responsive smile of greeting touched his lips. But something in his manner caused her to stare at him, perplexed. He seemed strangely triumphant as he stood there, as if half expecting some form of surrender.

And then he sighed. But he smiled too, and extended a hand to take her wrap as she came up the steps of the patio towards him.

'I've had the table set on the verandah at the side,' he told her. 'We can sit and look out across the strait.'

'That will be lovely.' She handed him her wrap, excitement in her veins and unattainable desires in her mind.

They went into the house; Jeanette had been there before, but she stood for a moment looking round. Magnolia walls and paintwork; a thick Turkish carpet of intricate design; white rugs and furniture in the modern style. Something missing ... the Meissen group and exquisite vases – And then she saw them, the Celadons which were set out on the cabinet where the Meissen had previously stood. With a little gasp of delight she moved nearer, but did not dare to touch.

'Like them?' His smile was faintly mocking. What was he thinking? *She* was vividly recalling his joke about her having to find herself a husband with a ready-made collection of Celadons. 'I had these few sent out from England.'

'They're beautiful!' She almost ached to touch the bowl nearest to her and she looked up. It was an automatic gesture, rather like a child seeking permission to do something it knew very well was forbidden. Craig laughed at her expression and told her to go ahead and pick it up.

'I daren't, but I'll just touch it.'

Craig picked it up and handed it to her. She knew she was holding about a thousand pounds in her hands. A thousand pounds. .... How could one value such beauty? If it were broken a thousand pounds could probably buy another – but no money in the world could replace it. When once a thing like this was broken it was lost for ever.

'Mark told me about your collection. ...' She caressed it almost lovingly. 'This is the first time I've touched one.'

Eventually he took it from her and, replacing it, he picked up another.

'I like this one; it's smaller, but the colour is quite unbelievable, don't you agree?'

Jeanette nodded, catching her breath. It was not just the colour or the shape which dazzled her, but also the great age of the bowl.

'The ninth century?'

'Yes – it's about eleven hundred years old.'

Jeanette sighed and replaced it; they stood by the cabinet for a while, talking, and then Craig's Turkish housekeeper announced that dinner was ready.

The sun had dropped and the enormous eastern moon had appeared to light up the strait and the hills across on the Asiatic shore. It was all so familiar to Jeanette by this time, and still she found it new and exciting.

Even when dinner was over they lingered there, sometimes talking, sometimes silent. The time flew and Jeanette felt a queer sense of loss when Craig said it was time he took her home. The evening was gone; she had only the memory.

The following day he called for her early. They both had shopping to do, so they decided this should be done first. Then they would have lunch in the city and go up in the afternoon to Eyüp, one of the most important places of Moslem pilgrimages.

Jeanette had made no definite date with Çetin, but she thought he might be free, in which case he would be almost sure to call, so she rang him to say she would be out for the whole of the day. Naturally surprised, he asked where she was going. Jeanette told him and when next he spoke his tone was almost savage.

'It's him again! Is he forcing you to go or are you going of your own free will?'

'Certainly I'm going of my own free will, Çetin.' She was determined to be patient, realizing that his anger stemmed from jealousy. Moreover, she must avoid any unpleasantness, owing to Çetin's friendship for Gwen and Sally, and all the rest of the crowd. 'I've already told you that Craig can't influence my actions.'

'He has before – and he's doing so now! If he hadn't come along you'd have been going out with me!'

'No, Çetin. I had already made up my mind to tell you that I didn't want to go out with you again. I'm sorry –

very sorry.' She felt convinced now that her suspicions had some foundation. Çetin would not have been content to let their relationship remain on a purely friendly basis.

'You're telling me that you never want to see me again?' His voice was low now, and knife-edged.

'Don't be silly; of course I shall see you. We'll all be going around together again just as soon as Sally and Gwen return. It's just that I don't think it is . . . wise for you and me to go out on our own.' That wasn't the whole truth, but she could scarcely say she found no enjoyment in going around with him. She wasn't being very tactful, even so, but Çetin was making things difficult for her. Also, she was seized by a strange uneasiness, an uneasiness that almost amounted to fear. She saw Çetin now, not as he'd been on the night he declared his love, but as he was when first they had set out on the climbing expedition – ruthless, almost cruel. This strange fear caused her hand to tremble, and as the receiver shook she chided herself for her stupidity. What harm could Çetin possibly do to her?

Even as she asked herself that question she heard his voice again, still low, but sounding almost evil, and her apprehension grew.

'When can I see you, Jeanette?'

She hesitated, finding herself cautiously searching for words which would mollify while at the same time leaving him in no doubt as to her determination not to see him again until they resumed the practice of going about in a crowd.

'I don't know when I shall be in, Çetin.' She looked up as Craig passed the window. He raised a hand and smiled, then passed on and she heard him enter through the side door. 'We really must leave it until the others come back,' she told Çetin hurriedly. 'Please don't come here, I really mean that.' She waited a few seconds, but, as he did not reply, she said good-bye and replaced the receiver.

There was a worried frown on her face as she joined

Craig in the sitting-room; he looked at her searchingly but, to her relief, made no comment.

Murad, brown-faced and stolid, drove them into the city. As usual, chaos reigned supreme on the Galata Bridge, but Jeanette never seemed to mind the delay, for there was always so much to see. Before them was a little cart, loaded so that it seemed to sag under the weight, and drawn by a tired-looking horse whose driver appeared to have fallen asleep. Trudging along the sides of the bridge were the *hamals*, harnessed human beasts of burden carrying their fantastic loads, their backs bent double. On the side, too, the familiar spectacle of the Anatolian peasant with his wives in the rear, the numerous boot-blacks, the usual array of fish being sold, freshly caught by the fishermen sitting around in their boats tied up at the side of the bridge.

Later, they walked on to the bridge; this was even more exciting to Jeanette, and this time she had no anxiety about Craig's being bored. He seemed quite willing to stop and stare just whenever she wanted to, although he did remark, with a hint of amusement, that he would have expected her to be used to it all by now.

'I don't come into the old city that often,' she said, and after a slight hesitation, 'Can we go to the Grand Bazaar when we've done our essential shopping?'

'I suspect you're plotting an antique hunt—' He took her arm, urging her to one side as a grinning, toothless fishmonger thrust a *lüfer* almost into her face. 'I wasn't thinking of spending the full day in the city, you know.'

She glanced up quickly, struck by the indulgent note in his voice. His dark eyes smiled at her teasingly.

'It's so tempting, Craig. Don't you find it impossible to come away, once you're there? Don't you feel excited when you've suddenly come across a bargain?' Even as she said that she thought of the Celadons. Craig would undoubtedly scorn some of the things she collected. 'I expect you have no need to search for bargains,' she added, while at the same time thinking that much of the pleasure must be lost if you could always afford to buy just whatever you desired.

'Now why should you think that? Of course I need to search for bargains – everyone does.'

'But . . . the Celadons?'

'My grandmother's collection mostly. Bought long before prices soared to what they are today. I myself have added a few, but they are now so rare, and so expensive, that my collection will grow very slowly, I'm afraid.'

The shopping completed, and their purchases taken back to the car, Jeanette and Craig made their way to the Bazaar. It was a city in itself, having grown from a small market built by the Sultan in the fifteenth century. There were numerous alleyways and streets, all narrow and pulsating with life. Stalls and shops lined these alleys, their goods spilling over into the roadway. Often their proprietors would be sitting together in groups, smoking *narghiles* and watching the passers by without any apparent interest.

'They don't look as if they want to sell anything,' Jeanette remarked as they jostled their way between baskets and ropes, carpets and leather goods – to say nothing of the masses of tourists who now added their numbers to the already overcrowded city.

But if these particular groups of traders could sit contentedly smoking and chatting, it wasn't so with many of the others. Runners came up by the dozen, demanding to know what they wanted, and literally ushering them into the Inner Market where the dealers came out to meet them. At one time, as the crowd thickened, it seemed impossible that they would not be separated, and Craig took Jeanette's hand.

'What would you like?' he asked when, having managed successfully to convince the various traders that they were 'only looking' they found themselves unmolested and free to wander in peace. 'How about some jade?' He drew her towards a shop where, on the stall outside, there were some lovely jade and alabaster figures and vases.

She felt suddenly shy. It seemed wrong, somehow, for Craig to be buying her a present. But he had picked up a charming little Buddha which she had already noticed. Smilingly he held it out to her, asking if she liked it. She paused for a long moment.

'Yes, I do, but—'

'We'll have it, then.' Without further ado he paid for it and they were soon on their way again, into the alley of jewellers. The windows dazzled, packed to capacity with glittering gold and silver and precious gems. There was a row of these shops, so brilliantly lighted that the heat from the windows could be felt in the middle of the alleyway.

'Are we going over there?' asked Jeanette, glancing at her companion uncertainly.

'You're determined to search through the junk?'

'Not if you don't want to,' she answered agreeably. But Craig steered her to where she wanted to go. They made slow progress, stepping over a miscellany of clothes and shoes and household articles scattered on the pavement, side-stepping the *hamel* laden with a great bale of cloth, evading the rather dignified approach of the young stall-holder bent on making a sale. It was excitingly oriental and colourful, teeming with movement amid a confusion of sounds.

'Oh, dear,' exclaimed Jeanette after about half an hour's futile search among the 'junk', 'I think I've had enough. It's so hot!' She put a hand to her brow, felt its moisture and brought out a handkerchief. She was limping slightly; she hadn't realized until Craig abruptly remarked on it.

'Is it aching?' he added, a frown darkening his face.

'No, I don't think so.' Odd, but she could feel it now that Craig had mentioned it.

'It must be; otherwise you wouldn't be limping.' His tone had changed, hinting at anger.

Jeanette bit her lip, aware that he was thinking of the way she had ignored his advice about climbing with

Çetin. And that must naturally lead his thoughts on to her letting him down over the book. It must appear, she mused dejectedly, that she had preferred to go with Çetin. Looking up into his stern set face, she wished she could explain. But she could hardly enlighten him as to the real reason for her change of mind about going with him to the island.

His manner remained stiff and cool as, after getting into the car, they were driven back across the bridge and along the Istiklâl Caddesi to Taksim Square.

They had lunch at the famous Park Hotel and as the meal progressed Craig's manner relaxed, but he did seem anxious about the afternoon's trip to Eyüp, because of course there was a hill to climb.

'I shall be all right,' she assured him. 'It was the heat that made me tired.'

'It wasn't the heat that made you limp.' He picked up the menu, but wasn't reading it because he added, while still appearing to be scanning it, 'You'll have to take care. Is the doctor satisfied? He's not expecting any complications?'

She shook her head.

'No, he says it will ache for a while, but there's nothing to worry about.'

That appeared to satisfy him, but he warned her that if the leg continued to ache she must tell him and they'd go home at once.

'This rest will do it good. It's nothing serious, Craig.' She watched him as he sat reading the menu. The set line of his mouth had softened and she knew that his concern for her was genuine. He became aware of her intent gaze and looked up for a second and down again, returning his attention to the menu. She caught her breath. How handsome he was! She fell to thinking of Diane, seeing her and Craig dancing together and recalling that she had thought how well matched they were. And for the first time Jeanette felt a tinge of envy. The next moment she shook it off, ashamed. After what Diane had been through, after her great sacrifices for others she deserved a man like Craig, a man who would care for her and make up for all she had missed.

Jeanette turned, to stare out of the window, but she was only vaguely aware of the view; the mouth of the Golden Horn, the slender minarets of St. Sophia and the Sultan Ahmet Mosque and, away in the far distance, across the smooth dark Sea of Marmara, the shadowed outlines of the Princes' Islands. For she still retained the mental vision of Diane, laughing up at Craig as in perfect harmony they glided across the dance floor.

How soon, she wondered, before Diane and Craig were married?

The sudden stab of pain in her heart was almost physical; there was a heaviness behind her eyes, the weight of tears suppressed.

Unexpectedly Craig spoke, the sharpness of his tone jerking her back to her surroundings.

'My dear child, what are you thinking about to make you look like that?'

Startled, she brought her gaze away from the window, forcing a smile.

'I was ... miles away.' She even managed to laugh, though rather shakily. 'Have you noticed the view, Craig? It's – it's breathtaking!'

He looked at her, his eyes kindling, then he gave an exasperated sigh and almost snapped,

'Miles away, were you? In England, by any chance?'

'In England?' She stared at him. 'What do you mean?' Such an odd thing to say. ... Had he, judging from her expression, assumed she was thinking of Ned? But why this anger? Why should Craig care if she sat there thinking about the past? Without conscious effort she found herself recalling other occasions when his anger had puzzled her. She remembered also those rare and precious moments when their intimacy was so profound that it seemed no two people could ever be closer. Her heart throbbed. Diane was forgotten as, confounded by the hint of an idea that had crossed her mind, she began to speak, her lips moving with difficulty, her words a mere whisper. 'No, Craig, I . . . I wasn't in—'

'Never mind,' he cut in abruptly. 'Tell me what you want, and let's eat.'

Their drive to Eyüp took them once more across the Galata Bridge, past the Camii of Rustem Pasha, with its vast dome and shining minarets, past Ayvansaray, the narrow part of the Golden Horn, where ferrymen waited to take people across the smooth and tideless water. The mighty land walls of Byzantium, vast and colourful, seemed to sway in the quivering haze cast by the intense brilliance of the sun.

And then they came to the Moslem shrine, the *turbé* of Abu Eyüp, disciple of Mahomet and the Prophet's personal standard-bearer. The change was staggering; from the throng of moving, living things they passed into a fantastic city of the dead, fantastic because of its orderliness, for the dead were lying in rows, and sometimes in squares, massed together.

'All these graves!' Jeanette stared unbelievingly around her. 'There must be miles of them!'

Craig went on to explain that because Eyüp was so good, so holy, the desire of all Moslems was to be buried as close to him as possible.

Strangely, there was nothing macabre about this vast city of the dead; on the contrary, perhaps owing to hundreds of years of veneration by devout pilgrims from all over the Moslem world, there was spread around an atmosphere of peace similar to that of which Jeanette had been so profoundly conscious on first entering the Mosque of Sultan Ahmet.

'As we are infidels, we cannot enter the *turbé*,' Craig informed her with a wry smile. 'You'll have to be content with looking through the grating.'

They then made their way through the forest of graves to Pierre Loti's café where, sitting apart from the tourists, several men were drinking coffee or smoking *narghiles*. Craig, Jeanette noticed, was watching her movements closely and she was not surprised when, after they had found seats, he inquired if her leg were aching.

'No, it's fine,' she answered truthfully, smiling at him across the table. The tension that had come between them at lunch time was gone and Craig seemed just as determined as she to enjoy their outing.

They sipped their coffee, sitting outside the café. The proprietor spoke to them, rattling off some well-rehearsed details of Pierre Loti's association with the place, and informing them that souvenirs of him could be bought at most reasonable prices. Craig thanked him politely but refused his offer of the souvenirs.

Below them Istanbul shimmered in the heat, a magic, semi-oriental city like something out of The Arabian Nights. In the other direction, away across the wide expanse of tombs, lay the Sweet Waters of Europe where, it was believed, the first settlement was made by the Dorian tribes almost three thousand years ago.

The sun was beginning to set as they drove back to Ortaköy. Craig had said earlier that they would dine out, but they had had a tiring day, with the heat and the walking, and he suggested they have dinner again at his house, and he would take Jeanette home immediately afterwards.

About this arrangement she had no complaint; nothing could round off her day more pleasantly than to dine alone with Craig. Again it was an informal meal, taken on the verandah, with the flower-scented air all around and the starlit sky above.

She thought, as she got into bed, that she would always remember it as one of the happiest days of her life but, putting out a hand to snap off the bed lamp, she caught sight of the little jade Buddha that Craig had bought for her. A sickening despair took possession of her; she turned her face into the pillow, trying to ease the throbbing pain behind her eyes.

CHAPTER EIGHT

DURING the next few days Jeanette and Craig covered hundreds of miles. Their travels took them over to the quieter, rather rustic eastern shore of the Bosphorus; to Scutari where thousands of Anatolian peasants lived in their picturesque wooden *yalis*. They visited beauty spots and palaces, quaint waterside cafés where they could choose their lobster, still alive, and eat it less than an hour later. They climbed the hill at Kanlica at seven one evening to watch the fantastic sunset, then sat idling in a village café eating the *yoğurt* for which Kanlica is famous. They spent an idyllic afternoon exploring the Sweet Waters of Asia, that playground of Ottoman society, haunt of the Sultans whose guests, rowed upstream in ornately gilded barges manned by six liveried *kayikei*, would picnic beneath the shade of the trees.

In the evenings Jeanette and Craig would visit a night club or restaurant. One evening they went to a concert at the Italian Consulate and Jeanette was introduced to several people who knew Craig. She was eyed with interest and surprise, for, of course, Craig usually went to such functions either alone or with a man friend.

On the Sunday evening they decided to stay at home, and Craig was Jeanette's guest for dinner. He arrived late, full of apologies but explaining that he had had to take his housekeeper to her mother's. The old woman was nearly ninety and had a serious fall.

'She'll need her daughter's care for some time, I'm afraid,' he told Jeanette.

'So you're without anyone to look after you?'

He shrugged.

'I expect Murad can turn his hand to a bit of cleaning; as for the cooking ... well, I'm not in very much,' he added with a smile.

She would have liked to offer her help in keeping the house tidy, but she refrained. It seemed altogether too intimate. She would also have liked to suggest his taking his meals with her, when they weren't going out, but she was not at all sure that he intended staying much longer in Istanbul. For the last two days he had often been deeply preoccupied, and once or twice he had spoken his thoughts aloud, talking about his book, and it was not difficult to see that he was ready – even anxious – to begin working on it again.

Would he go to Büyük Ada? she wondered with a sudden access of desolation. Under the circumstances it seemed the most sensible thing to do, for then he would have his two Turkish servants to look after him.

They were sitting on the patio, having drinks while waiting for the dinner to be served, and as she looked at his face, trying to read his thoughts, she just had to say:

'Aren't you going to work on your book, Craig? I mean, I've had the impression lately that you're keen on doing so. Also, if you were at the *yali* you would have someone to look after you.' She was unaware of the tremor in her voice, the hint of dejection in the droop of her shoulders.

Metat came to announce that the dinner was ready. Craig waited until he had gone again and then said curiously,

'Do you want me to go, Jeanette?'

'No, no, I don't.' The words came swiftly, without thought. She flushed and added, 'But you did want to finish the book by the end of the year – and you've neglected it because of me.'

'Haven't you enjoyed this past week?'

'You know I have.' Her glance held gratitude – gratitude not only for the excursions, but for the memories. Naturally she could not tell him that.

'So have I.' He rose, picking up their glasses. 'The book has not, therefore, been neglected because of you.' He gazed down at her; she sensed the rebuke his silence implied and her flush deepened. She was just asking herself if she would ever understand him when he said, with that hint of asperity she had come to know so well, 'You're a strange girl, Jeanette. I find it quite impossible to fathom your way of thinking.'

They went in to dinner; the old easy manner returned and later when they again went out to the patio Jeanette felt oddly at peace, even though she was at the same time profoundly aware of Craig's nearness, of the overwhelming influence and magnetism of his presence. She leant back in her chair; the soft glow from the lanterns in the trees cast lights into her hair and her eyes. She saw Craig regarding her with a strange expression and sent him a spontaneous smile.

He caught his breath, hesitated, and then,

'I intended never to ask you again, Jeanette, but ... will you come to Büyük Ada with me? You were right when you said you thought I was keen to continue with the book. I feel somehow that it will – flow now.' Another hesitation. 'I should very much appreciate your help.'

She was no longer enveloped in peace; her heart raced madly and she found herself trembling with excitement. To be with Craig for several weeks, on a romantic island in the Sea of Marmara....

'I – Craig, I don't know. ...' Even as her sanity returned he was speaking again, speaking in gentle tones, persuasively and with a faint expression of urgency in his voice.

'I suppose you're thinking we could do it just as well here, but it's not so. I've tried. The environment's right, somehow, on the island.' He smiled at her then and added, 'And this *is* our vacation; we wouldn't be writing all the time. We could swim, and perhaps sail sometimes.'

All so attractive, all so tempting – but the image of Diane rose between them, Diane who would soon be Craig's wife. Jeanette's mind was in a turmoil; she lived again through that painful conversation with Mrs. Fleming, the conversation that had led to the discovery of her own feelings for Craig. Mrs. Fleming would not be pleased to know that she was at the *yali* with her son.

'I'll have to think.' How desperately she wanted to go! The madness took possession again. Why not? What had she to lose? Craig would welcome her help; and if she loved him, then why shouldn't she help him? And why shouldn't she seize the opportunity of having him all to herself for a few weeks? For that was all she would have – to last for the rest of her life. This thought hurt, hurt unbearably, and her eyes were bright as she looked across at him.

She put trembling hands to her temples. How could she keep her secret if they were to work and play, and live side by side. It wasn't humanly possible. After that admission her decision was easy. She knew, as she looked into his eager face, that once she refused it would be the end, the end of their friendship. She was also convinced he would go to Büyük Ada alone.

Well, the sooner the break came the sooner the wound would begin to heal.

'I'm sorry, Craig, but I don't want to go to the island.' She didn't know what words to use, and her voice sounded sharp, because of the dryness in her throat. She saw him stiffen. Her refusal was a blow to his pride. He regretted having asked her. She saw a pulsating movement in his temple, but it was his icy expression which held her. His voice was like flint.

'That appears to be conclusive enough. I don't think there's anything more to be said.' He stood up as he spoke, and she whispered, almost against her will,

'Are you going to the island?'

'First thing in the morning.'

And then she was alone. For a moment the garden was still and silent. And then a cool, flower-scented breeze touched her burning forehead, and from afar came the clear sweet song of a nightingale. With a trembling little sob Jeanette rose to her feet and went into the house.

Craig had been gone almost a week when Çetin called. It had been a week of loneliness for Jeanette, comparable in pain and heartache to those months immediately following her fiancé's death. It had been a time of conflict, too. She seemed to be torn apart, one moment wishing she could have another chance and accept Craig's offer, and the next moment knowing full well that she had acted wisely. The strain of this conflict left her weak; she had become pale and tired-looking and when Çetin appeared she felt she had neither the strength nor the inclination even to speak to him. She was angry that he should call, but she had to remember that he was a friend of Sally and Gwen, and she endeavoured to hide her feelings.

She smiled as she asked him in and invited him to sit down. He sprawled in the chair, looking up at her with narrowed eyes.

'So you're not out with him today?' His mouth was tight and his lips were curved into an almost ugly line. Jeanette wondered how she had ever come to regard him as handsome. He appeared to be under some kind of stress, seething beneath a façade of mild civility. For some quite incomprehensible reason her heart began to flutter, and it flashed through her mind that Metat was having his afternoon break and would be in a café somewhere with Murad, and that Mrs. Baydur was out shopping.

'No, Çetin,' she said guardedly. 'Not today.'

'Not tomorrow, either. Why has he gone to Büyük Ada?'

She glanced down at him, startled.

'How do you know that Craig has gone to the island?'

'His yacht isn't there.'

Of course. She hadn't thought of that. Çetin was waiting for an answer to his question and she told him that Craig had decided to do some work on his book.

His manner changed; his tones were softer and faintly perceptive.

'Have you quarrelled with him?'

'No!' she returned emphatically. 'Why should you ask that?'

He moved in his chair, sitting up straight.

'Rumour has it,' he said, 'that Craig Fleming is in love with some married woman. Her husband's gravely ill and they're just waiting for the poor devil to die.'

Jeanette flinched. How people twisted the truth! It hurt her intolerably to hear Craig spoke of like this.

'There's more to it than most people realize, Çetin,' was all she would say.

'Perhaps,' he conceded, shrugging. 'But they will marry when this woman becomes a widow?' It was more a statement than a question; Jeanette had to agree with him, but her manner remained non-committal.

'Then you do realize that you're wasting your time in running after him?'

'I don't run after him!' she denied, flushing hotly. Was that how it appeared? Were others thinking the same thing?

'Maybe I shouldn't have said that,' he apologized, but added, 'Nevertheless you do prefer his company to mine.' A sulky note entered his voice and again she had to pity him, wondering how deeply he cared and whether his suffering were as great as hers.

He seemed to be waiting, as if hoping she might deny the truth of his words, and when she remained silent his mouth became once more set and hard.

His attitude was difficult to read. Jeanette had not had much to do with men like Çetin; he belonged to the new Turkey, to the youth of the country. He had never displayed the rather servile manner which seemed to come naturally to the older men employed by people like Mark and Craig. There was an arrogance about Çetin which she had always disliked and yet, strangely, she could not resent.

He spoke softly, asking her how long Craig had been gone.

'I noticed last night that his yacht wasn't there,' he continued, 'but I haven't been this way for three or four days.'

'He went last Tuesday – a week tomorrow.'

'You've been on your own?' His voice was edged with bitterness. 'You could have rung me.'

'There was nothing to ring you for.' She looked at him apologetically, reluctant to add to his unhappiness and yet wishing he would try to accept the situation. 'There can't be anything between you and me – please don't keep on hoping.'

'You ... won't come out with me this evening? We could dine and dance. I promise I won't say a word out of place.' He was pleading, in spite of her efforts.

She shook her head in desperation, unable to cope. The strain of her own position had frayed her nerves and she felt that if Çetin persisted she would burst into tears.

'Please go,' she begged. 'I just want to be left alone.'

'Left alone?' He stood up and came close to her, his face dark with suppressed anger. 'It's not natural for a woman to want to be alone! It's him – why didn't *he* leave you alone? Why did he have to come along and spoil everything? You were quite happy, going around with me—'

'No, no, I wasn't. I knew it wouldn't work, because I felt nothing for you—' She broke off, the colour leaving her face as she saw his expression. Her glance fluttered to the window. How long would it be before Mrs. Baydur returned?

'You could have cared – if he hadn't come between us?'

There was an evil gleam in his eyes and Jeanette took an instinctive step backwards. The action had the effect of releasing some pent-up emotion in Çetin. He seemed almost primitive, and her voice became husky with fear as she spoke.

'Çetin ... neither of us is enjoying this conversation, and – and I have asked you to go. Please do so ... n-now.'

He stared at her, his nostrils flared and then, before

she knew what he was about to do he had seized her arm, holding it in a brutal grip as he pulled her towards him.

'Let me go—'

'I want you,' he said savagely. 'You're the first woman I've ever loved – and I won't let you go!' He laughed at her struggles and then his expression became evil again as he took her face in a cruel grip, forcing her head back. She was paralysed with fear, terrified she would faint, and again she struggled desperately, trying to free herself.

His mouth was close to hers and with a shuddering moan of despair she waited to feel the savage pressure of his lips.

And then she was free. Dazed, she watched Çetin go staggering back, regaining his balance only just in time to prevent himself from crashing into the wall.

'Get out!' Craig's voice was a whip-lash and his face was white with fury. 'Get out before I throw you out!'

Çetin straightened up, his lips drawn back into a snarl as he made a movement as if to strike Craig. Craig's eyes were narrowed and challenging; he waited, but Çetin, thinking better of it, moved to the window through which Craig had entered.

'I'll go – but I'm not saying I won't be back.'

'You'll get more than you bargain for if you do come back.' Craig's voice was low now and even. 'Take my advice, Rustem, and keep away.'

'Are you going to stand guard over her all the time?' No mistaking the sneer on Çetin's lips or the arrogance of his tone.

Craig merely looked at him contemptuously, but his attitude was a threat and after a glance of hatred Çetin turned and stepped through the window. The next moment his car was roaring along the drive, lost in a cloud of dust.

Silently, Craig and Jeanette looked at one another. By what miracle he had so opportunely arrived she did not know, but it was enough that he should be here, even though his eyes smouldered and his lips were compressed into a thin, tight line.

'Thank you, Craig,' she faltered, moving with difficulty to the couch. Her legs were so weak they could scarcely support her, and her heart pounded so madly that she felt almost sick. 'Metat and Mrs. Baydur went out. . . .'

Craig ignored that.

'How often has he been here during the past week?' he demanded, fully aware of her trembling, and the brightness of her eyes.

'This is the first time.'

'Has he made love to you before?'

'Certainly not!' Her cheeks flamed. 'And he wasn't doing so now!'

'Don't tell me that little scene hasn't had some sort of preliminary.' The hint of contempt in his voice brought the tears. She put her head in her hands and wept. He did not speak, but waited for the nervous tension to pass. When at last she looked up, drying her eyes, his face had a softened quality, but he still appeared more angry and impatient than she had ever seen him.

'I didn't mean to cry. . . .' Involuntarily she pressed one tightly closed fist to her heart as if to quieten its unnatural thudding. She looked up at him gravely. 'How do you come to be here? I thought you would be staying at the *yali* for at least a month.'

'I'd left some important notes behind. Murad was supposed to have put them in my case and obviously forgot. I thought I could manage without them, but I was just wasting time, so I decided to come back and get them.'

That did not explain why he was here, and she looked at him questioningly. He spoke with obvious reluctance, after a long and brooding silence.

'I thought I'd come over and see how you were – knowing you're on your own.'

'That was kind of you, Craig.' She was sure he let fall a little sigh of exasperation at her words, but there was

nothing in his expression to support this. 'You're returning to the island immediately?'

'Later this evening.' The merest pause. 'And you're
coming with me, whether you like it or not.'

'Oh, but I—'

'You're not staying here alone – not with Çetin in that
mood.' He watched her, expecting a protest, and went on
with swiftly rising anger, 'What would Mark think if I
were to leave you, knowing the danger you're in? You're
going to do as I say, Jeanette, and I don't want any
further argument!'

She hadn't argued, but she didn't tell him so, for she
was sure he was in no mood to pay attention to unimportant statements like that.

She had to agree that it was unwise to remain here, for
she was sure Çetin would return once Craig had again
departed for the island. On the other hand, it was also
unwise for her to stay with Craig at the *yali,* and although
uncomfortably aware that it was not the thing to do, she
tentatively suggested she stay at Craig's house here in
Ortaköy.

'Çetin wouldn't know where I was, so he couldn't
annoy me.'

'Have you forgotten my housekeeper is away?'

'Of course she is. Yes, I'd forgotten. I can't very well
stay with only Murad there.'

'And it wouldn't be quite the thing if I remained at
home. In any case, I have no wish to do so. You're
coming to Büyük Ada.' He looked past her, to the clock.
'I'll stay until Metat returns and then I'll leave you to
pack. Can you wait for your dinner until we arrive at the
yali?'

She nodded, all resistance leaving her. It seemed she
was fated to be with Craig on the island, and she
resignedly accepted her fate, too spent to enter into an
argument which, in any case, would prove to be futile.

Jeanette lay on the sand, her hands propped behind her

head, gazing dreamily out to sea. Craig lay on a chair beside her, his eyes closed.

It was nearly three weeks since they had left Istanbul, sailing to the island in the cool of a July evening, with the playful porpoises all around, and the dome and minarets of St. Sophia slipping away into the distance. For Jeanette it had been a time of pleasure and pain, of alternating happiness and dejection. Each morning they worked on the book; each afternoon they would go on to the beach, Craig's private little beach close to the landing-stage where his yacht was moored, and lie in the sun or swim in the warm blue waters of Marmara. Then there would be afternoon tea up at the *yali* or in one of the gay little cafés along the quay. Occasionally they would hire one of the two-horse buggies and make the five-mile circuit of the island, or go on a sleepy ride through the pine woods or to the top of some hill where they would loiter awhile to enjoy the superb view over to the other islands of the Princes' group.

In the evening they might be invited, by the owner of a nearby *yali*, to a barbecue on the beach. They would cook their food on a charcoal stove and eat it under a moonlit sky, with the tropical breeze warmed by the sea, drifting caressingly on to the shore. Craig in turn organized his own barbecue and Jeanette sent out the invitations and then helped generally to make the party a success. At other times they would dine out, in a restaurant, mingling with the tourists, and the wealthy Greek and Turkish families whose habit it was to come to the island for the whole of the summer. Or they might dine alone, with the table set out under lantern-hung trees in the beautiful garden of the *yali*. At all these times Jeanette took what fate had to offer and the resulting heartaches were determinedly ignored. But often she would lie awake at night, thinking of Craig, and the way he was, quite often, as attentive as a lover. And she would wonder how she could now live without him. Her mind would be tortured by the picture of Diane receiving all these attentions, and more tenderly given, for, of course, she would be Craig's wife.

Jeanette sat up as a motor launch skimmed the waves; there was a gay greeting from those on board, and she responded, her call awakening Craig from his half sleep. They both watched the launch, owned by a family who lived further along the beach. They were Turkish, and had become friendly with Craig just after they bought the white-painted, high-storied *yali* three years ago.

The launch became a toy on the horizon and Jeanette turned, aware of Craig's regard. Their eyes met, and smiled. A surge of happiness swept through her. Nothing seemed to matter but the present. Even though their stay on the island was coming to an end, there were still five days to go and she would not allow her thoughts to drift any further than that.

Craig rose, and they wandered slowly up to the house. He too seemed happy, without a care in the world, and she felt gratified by the knowledge that she had contributed to this state of mind, for the book had gone very well indeed and Craig had asserted with confidence that it would be finished by Christmas.

'What do we do this evening?' he asked as they sat under the trees in the garden having their tea. 'Shall we eat out, or at home?'

'At home,' she said quickly, and he smiled at her eagerness.

'I prefer that, too,' he said. 'We can walk afterwards, if you like?'

She smiled and nodded.

'I'd like that.' Their walks were always pleasant, taken in the cool of the evening, and usually through the pine woods, away from the lights and the crowds.

On returning from their walk they stayed for a while outside the *yali*. There had been a sudden shower and the air smelled freshly of rain. Craig was in a strange mood – had been since dinner. He was neither distant nor very close. He seemed to have something on his mind; seemed filled with indecision. His carefree attitude of the afternoon had disappeared. Jeanette accepted his mood, having decided long ago that, as far as she was concerned, there would always be something enigmatical about Craig. She would never understand him. Wonderful though her stay on the island had been, she was ever conscious of Craig's varying moods. Often he had shown impatience, and on occasions she had detected a hint of mockery, and even contempt, beneath his apparently teasing manner. At other times his gentleness had brought tears to her eyes and with a sense of guilt she would find herself once more envying the woman he was soon to marry.

'Do you want to go in?' he asked at length.

Another evening gone. A tightness came to Jeanette's throat. If they went in now there would be the usual quick drink and they would go up to their rooms, Craig, she knew, to work mentally on his book, and she herself to lie awake also, but for quite another reason. She felt a sudden urgency to prolong the evening and she said quickly,

'It's so lovely out here. Can we stay for a little while longer?'

Her words had a strange effect on him; he obviously favoured the idea, and the indecision of a few moments ago disappeared. He took her arm and they wandered down the garden towards the little jetty where his yacht lay moored.

Jeanette sighed, realizing the futility of her endeavours. What was there to be gained by keeping him at her side for another hour?

They stood by the jetty, under a star-filled sky, watching the lights from the numerous little fishing boats bobbing about on the water. Craig's hand was still under her arm; his fingers moved almost caressingly. An automatic gesture, she knew, but she trembled under his touch.

'You're not cold?' he asked with gentle concern. 'Shall we go back?' She could only shake her head dumbly, again wondering what benefit she derived from keeping him here. He sensed her dejection and said unexpectedly, 'What is it, child? There are times – and this is one of them – when I gain the impression that you would like to weep on my shoulder.' Her eyes darted to his. Was it her own lack of caution? – or Craig's almost uncanny perception? 'Well—' he lifted an eyebrow quizzically, 'are you going to deny it?'

She shook her head, giving him a wan smile.

'I do sometimes feel – rather depressed,' and, immediately regretting her admission, 'But it soon passes.'

A fishing boat came near the shore, and Craig's attention appeared to be diverted for a moment.

'What have you to be depressed about? Can't you tell me?'

Tell him! she thought bleakly. He was the last person she could tell.

'It soon passes,' was all she could find to say, and he moved impatiently. The eagerness with which he had agreed to their staying out a while longer was replaced by an odd disappointment which puzzled her.

'But it returns.' He regarded her fixedly, his mouth tight. 'I don't expect you'll thank me for what I'm going to say, Jeanette, but I'm going to say it, all the same.' A slight hesitation and then, 'Mark has told me about what happened to your fiancé.' He paused again, for her reaction; she remained silent, waiting for him to continue. It was odd, she mused, that she was now prepared to talk about Ned, feeling no pain at reviving the memory. But her silence aroused his anger and his voice became cold and harsh. 'Are you intending to dwell on the past for the rest of your life?' he demanded. 'Do you think the man who loved you would want you to go on living with a men ?'

His words astonished her, for although he had always spoken his mind, she would not have expected him to be so forthright as this over what to him should have seemed a most delicate matter. But, strangely, she did not take exception to his outspokenness and her voice was quiet and serene when she spoke.

'I'm not, Craig.' She now wanted to confide in him, to tell him that the memory no longer hurt. 'I'm not; you see—'

'You are!' he exclaimed wrathfully. 'I'm not minimizing your sorrow, but it's almost four years since it happened. You can't live with it for ever!'

Why this increase of anger? His lack of patience hurt. He had no right to show impatience when he himself continued to live in the past. But as always he assumed the role of mentor, telling her what to do without any intention of following his own advice. Her eyelids pricked; she longed for a return of his gentle manner, and she said quietly,

'I'm not living in the past, Craig, although it may seem so to you—'

'Then why are you so dead set against marriage? You're obviously determined on a life of spinsterhood. Explain that, if, as you say, you're not living in the past?' His tones were quieter now, but no less impatient. The tears were on her lashes as she murmured huskily,

'I can't ever marry, Craig, not now. I can't tell you why, but it isn't – it isn't what you think.' Before she had even finished he was sighing impatiently, and she knew he had paid no attention to her last words. Not that it mattered, for she could not have explained further.

'Why . . .? I know why.' He shrugged an angry resignation. 'Very well, have it your own way. I'll neither offer advice nor even mention the matter again. Let's go back to the house.'

Dumbly she walked beside him, but they had not taken more than half a dozen steps when they both turned as a launch came up to the jetty. Murad jumped out and handed Craig a letter.

'From England,' Jeanette heard him say, and then began speaking in Turkish. But now and then Craig put in a word in English, obviously so that Jeanette could

131

understand the conversation. Murad had brought the letter because he thought it might be urgent, coming from England. It had arrived just about tea time, but Murad couldn't come earlier because he had had difficulty in borrowing a launch.

Craig thanked him and Murad was soon on his way again, speeding away across the dark waters.

Immediately on entering the sitting-room Craig opened the envelope and took out the letter. Jeanette stood there, her heart fluttering almost painfully as she watched his face.

'Roy – Diane's husband – died on Tuesday,' he told her, still staring at the letter. His face was set and grim, but there was a certain sadness in his expression, and also in his tone when he spoke. 'It's tragic, for he was a fine man, but . . . but it's a relief for everyone concerned.' He fell into a pensive silence, and, quietly, Jeanette bade him good night. He did not hear, and she turned and left the room.

She had little sleep, merely dozing now and then, between long hours of wakefulness, and at seven o'clock she decided to get up and take a walk along the shore. Her cardigan was in the sitting-room and she went to fetch it.

The letter lay open on the table, where Craig had left it on going to bed. Despite herself Jeanette found her eyes drawn to it.

'. . . on Tuesday. I am helping dear Diane, and soon we shall be coming over. I hope, my son, that you and she will now find happiness together. Diane never mentions your future together, and neither do you, but I know this is what you have both been waiting for—' Jeanette dragged herself away from the table, ashamed of her lapse, and took up her cardigan from the couch.

The beach was deserted; she walked slowly, seeing nothing. A breeze wafted in from the sea, but although it soothed the feverish heat of her brow it brought no relief to the persistent little throb of pain in her temples.

CHAPTER NINE

By the middle of September Jeanette was back at school, throwing herself into her job by day and into the gay round of parties and other entertainments in the evenings. Çetin still made up one of the crowd, though he rarely spoke to Jeanette and she knew that his interest had waned. Often he would ignore her altogether, not even asking for a dance, and although Sally and Gwen remarked on this, being plainly puzzled by the change in Çetin, Jeanette remained silent about what had happened during the holiday.

Diane had come over for a short stay, accompanied by Mrs. Fleming, but this was only by way of a break before plunging herself into the business of disposing of her husband's estate. From something Mark said soon after their arrival Jeanette concluded Diane was selling everything without delay.

'Then she's coming here – for good?' Her throat suddenly hurt, so that her words were scarcely audible. 'Will she and Craig be married here?'

'From what Craig's mother says they're to be married in England. Then they'll live here until Craig moves to Greece. He plans on settling on one of the islands there.'

'It seems odd,' she couldn't help saying, 'that Craig doesn't want to settle in England. After all, his mother has no one else in the world – at least, that's what Diane once told me.'

There was a slight hesitation before her brother spoke.

'Craig's mother is a very possessive woman, and a managing one. She's always suggesting to Craig that she knows what's best for him – and, as you can imagine,' he added with a grimace, 'he's not the man to tolerate anything like that. But I do know he has a deep affection for her, and would never deliberately hurt her feelings.'

Mark paused for a moment and Jeanette's thoughts went back to that night on the island when she and Craig had returned rather late from their walk. Craig's eyes had glinted when his mother glanced at the clock, but when he spoke there was no indication of any anger or resentment in his voice. 'I really believe that's the reason he came away from England in the first place – in order to get away from her. Craig has his own subtle way of handling his affairs, so that she has never guessed at the truth. Had he set up his own establishment in England it would have been clear that he didn't want to live with her. That would obviously have upset her, and I imagine, knowing her, that it could have caused a deep and lasting rift. Naturally, Craig wouldn't want anything like that to happen.'

'Do you – do you think it's definite that Craig and Diane will marry?' Jeanette spoke with difficulty, flushing as her brother threw her a flickering, sidelong glance. 'I mean – you once said that – that people change. . . .' Why refer to that? she asked herself, with swift impatience. It had merely been an incidental remark passed by her brother, expressing his opinion at the time, a vague opinion which he had immediately dismissed as of no importance.

'I think it's very definite that they'll marry,' he replied, ignoring her last remark. 'Mrs. Fleming couldn't talk of anything else when I was over there last evening; besides, you've only to see Diane and Craig together.' Jeanette was struck by the odd note in his voice. It brought to mind that element of compassion that had entered into his manner immediately on her regaining consciousness after the climbing accident. But there was something else in Mark's voice now, a sort of despair, an almost bitter resignation. 'And that reminds me,' he added suddenly, 'you and I are going over to Craig's place for dinner tomorrow evening. He phoned this morning and I accepted on your behalf. You hadn't arranged anything important?'

She shook her head. Mark knew that her evenings were spent in a frivolous round of parties and dances. She guessed at his disapproval, and was hurt by it, but how could she explain the reason for embarking on this totally aimless existence? But she wished Mark hadn't accepted the invitation for her. She had seen very little of Craig since their return from the island, having determinedly avoided him on all possible occasions, and she had hoped, more than ever, to avoid him while Diane was here. There was no sense in adding to her misery by seeing him and Diane together. Nor had she any particular inclination to see Mrs. Fleming again, for she sensed her dislike, even though she could find no reason for it. However, Mark had accepted, and Jeanette could think of no feasible excuse for declining the invitation.

Diane and Craig were standing on the patio, very close, their faces glowing in the softly-shaded light, and a stab of pain caught at Jeanette's heart as she recalled that other evening, when she had come alone, and when Craig had stood there alone, waiting for her. So intimate a meal it had been, and they had remained on the verandah long after it was over, their thoughts seeming to be in complete harmony as they sat there, under a star-filled sky, their quiet conversation often interrupted by long silences when they would just stare out across the strait to the distant twinkling lights along the eastern shore of the Bosphorus.

And now Craig stood there with Diane, both appearing so happy, and so suited to one another. No doubt about it, Diane was incredibly beautiful, and she had such an attractive way of looking up at Craig, which she did now, after smiling a welcome to Jeanette and Mark as they approached the steps of the patio.

Craig bent his head to whisper something to Diane, and they both laughed softly. What was it like, Jeanette wondered, to be free to express one's love after years of enforced restraint? Jeanette was conscious of Craig's eyes upon her, and of the movement of his arm as he reached down to take Diane's hand in his. In spite of herself she gave a trembling little sigh, and at that moment her brother's arm came round her as they mounted the steps of the patio. It was an automatic gesture of guidance which any man would extend to a woman he happened to be escorting, a gesture of which Mark himself was probably unaware. Yet it brought her a much needed comfort and she turned to give him a smile of gratitude and thanks.

Throughout the meal Jeanette was constantly reminded of her brother's words, 'You've only to see Diane and Craig together'. If there had been a hint of doubt in her mind before, it was completely dispelled now, for Craig was all gentleness, all tender concern. Diane responded to his attentions with a loving smile, yet underneath it all Jeanette sensed a sadness about her and knew that although her husband's death had given her the freedom she desired, Diane did in fact experience a deep feeling of loss. How in keeping with her character — that she could genuinely mourn the loss of the man who had stood between her and Craig for so many years. Jeanette thought once more that it was no wonder Craig had waited so long and so patiently for the day when she would be his wife.

When the meal was over Mrs. Fleming, complaining of a headache, went up to her room for a rest, saying she would be down again later. The others went into the sitting-room for coffee and as Mark and Craig became engrossed in the subject of sailing, Jeanette and Diane sat together on the settee, conversing on rather trivial matters for a while. Jeanette several times tried to offer sympathy over Roy's death, having been unable to find a suitable opportunity during dinner, but again she experienced difficulty until Diane herself finally provided an opening.

'I love it here, and could do with another couple of weeks, but I must get back home — for a while at any rate. I suppose you know I'm selling my house — the whole of

Roy's estate, in fact?'

Jeanette nodded, taking advantage of the opening to express her regret and sympathy. Diane thanked her and although there was a distinct note of sadness in her voice, she did add that she was glad the end had come, for her husband's sake.

'He was in great pain, and it hurt us all to see him. He wanted to go – had wanted it for some considerable time.' She lapsed into silence, and Jeanette was reluctant to break into her thoughts. But after a while Diane spoke again, her glance flickering oddly as she half turned so as to face her companion. 'I hear that you once went through a sad time, too, Jeanette.'

The matter of her fiancé's death was brought into the conversation so subtly that Jeanette experienced no more than the merest sense of surprise.

'Did Craig tell you about it?' she asked, her glance flickering to him as he sat with Mark, on the other side of the room, deep in conversation.

'Mark told me, about eighteen months ago when we met by accident in a café. I didn't know you then, of course, though I knew, when we were at university together, that Mark had a kid sister.' She smiled, that enchanting smile that was now tinged with sorrow. 'Craig knows all about it, though—' She broke off, sending Jeanette a slanting glance, and then looking down again as if undecided about her next words.

'Mark told him about the way you feel – that you never intend to marry.' She turned impulsively. 'Do you resent my talking like this, Jeanette? I know we're not terribly well acquainted, but I'm sure we're going to be friends.'

'No, I don't mind your talking like this,' Jeanette replied, and she meant it. Whether or not they would be friends was uncertain for, convinced that she could not endure to see Craig and Diane married, Jeanette was already toying with the idea of breaking her contract and returning to England with her brother at Christmas. 'I don't know why Mark told Craig these things about me,' she added, faintly embarrassed.

'I expect it came out naturally, in the course of conversation. After all, Mark and Craig are very good friends – they certainly were in their younger days – and Mark probably felt he must explain why you were coming over here.'

'Craig – Craig knows the reason for my coming?' Mark must have told him every little detail, Jeanette concluded, not without surprise. While she owned that it was natural for Mark to have mentioned the tragedy of Ned's death, it seemed very odd that he should have related so many intimate details of her life to Craig. The only circumstances under which she could imagine his doing so were if he should be asked outright – and Craig certainly would not be interested enough to do that.

'Craig knows you came out here because you were so unhappy, that your brother suggested it, thinking it would help you to forget.' She paused, then added, 'But it hasn't helped you, has it, Jeanette?' Her voice was sweet, and low; Jeanette could not possibly take offence.

'Yes, it has helped, Diane, but. . . .'

'But what?' Still that low sweet tone, though it now contained a hint of persuasion, too. Jeanette felt choked; she could not explain to Diane, despite the distinct hint of encouragement, the unspoken assurance that she would find this girl a sympathetic listener. 'Perhaps you don't know it,' went on Diane at length, 'but Craig worries about you. He thinks you're a nice girl and it's a shame that you adopt this attitude towards marriage.'

He thought her a nice girl . . . and felt she should marry . . . Jeanette's lips quivered and for a moment recalled the many occasions when he had shown impatience with her. These had puzzled her at first, but gradually she had begun to suspect that they might have sprung from some knowledge of her past imparted to him by her brother. Her suspicions had been correct, as Diane's words now proved. She recalled his saying that Ned would not have wanted her to live in the past, to spoil her life by refusing to marry anyone else. Jeanette felt she fully understood now; Craig was just the sort of person who would have no patience with anyone who bemoaned their fate, who would not fight to lift themselves out of the rut of their misery and find the courage to make a new life.

Looking up, Jeanette realized that Diane was waiting patiently for some response to her comments, and she said, with a break in her voice, that she could never marry. A sudden frown crossed Diane's brow and she flicked a glance to Craig, who was still deep in conversation with Mark.

'I don't know why Craig should worry about me,' Jeannett added, noticing her glance and also remembering Diane's earlier statement. It seemed so very odd, sitting here, carrying on this sort of conversation with the girl whom Craig was soon to marry.

As for Diane herself, she was lost in thought and Jeanette knew she hadn't heard her last remark. The frown was still present on her brow and when at last she broke the silence her voice held an odd mixture of impatience and concern.

'My Roy,' she began, turning her attention once more to Jeanette, 'he loved me very much – and because he loved me, he wouldn't want me to go on and on, living with his memory. He would want me to find happiness. Your fiancé . . . do you really think he would want you to forfeit all that life has to offer? Would he wish you to renounce marriage?' She shook her head and added gently, 'Forgive my outspokenness, Jeanette, but I think the time has come for you to sort yourself out. Life has so much to offer. You can't go on like this; you're so young, and it isn't natural for you to persist in this resolution never to marry.'

But even before she had finished Jeanette was shaking her head.

'I can't explain, Diane,' she whispered huskily. 'I shall never marry, never. But I can't explain,' she said again. 'Not to you above all people.'

'Not to me?' Diane looked at her askance, the frown deepening. 'That's an odd thing to say, Jeanette.' Again her glance flickered to Craig; he looked up and smiled, affectionately. Diane seemed to give a deep and almost angry sigh.

'Do you really mean that?' she asked, and Jeanette nodded her head firmly.

'I mean it, Diane. I have no wish at all to get married.' A flicker of a smile touched her lips. 'It's kind of both you and Craig to be so interested in me, but there's no need. I'm – I'm quite content as I am.' She tried to sound convincing, tried to deepen her smile, but she knew she failed. However, to her relief Craig and Mark were both looking across, their own discussion at an end, and the two girls were drawn into a more casual conversation in which, now and then, Diane and Craig would indulge in some personal banter, teasing each other, as lovers will. Jeanette was beginning to wonder how she would get through the rest of the evening when Mark, catching her eye, said gently,

'You look tired, Jeanette. Would you like to go home?' He turned. 'You won't mind, will you, Craig?'

'It's far too early,' Diane put in, her eyes on Mark. 'Don't go yet – you're not really tired, are you, Jeanette?' she added, turning to her with a smile.

'I – well—' Was Diane merely being polite? – or was she genuinely wanting them to stay? It seemed very odd that she hadn't jumped at the chance of being alone with Craig. I would have done, Jeanette owned to herself. Aloud she said, 'I can't honestly say I'm tired.' She smiled wanly at Craig, who added his own request to that of Diane.

'That's settled, then,' declared Diane, embracing them all with that lovely smile. 'I don't know how everyone else feels, but I'm dying for some fresh air. Can we go for a walk, Craig?'

'It's too cold.' There was an almost icy wind blowing down from the Black Sea, he went on to say, and that appeared to be the end of the matter, as far as he was concerned. But Diane pouted, saying it wasn't too cold at all, and hinting that he was too lazy to bestir himself. This was a mood entirely new to Jeanette; her eyes were on Craig, watching intently for his reaction, though her thoughts had strayed to those times when, with her, he had arbitrarily brushed aside all opposition to his will.

But now, noting Diane's protesting gaze, and the almost childish pout of her pretty mouth, Craig smiled indulgently and made no further attempt to have his own way. How he must love her! For Jeanette knew for sure that it must go very much against the grain for Craig to submit to the will of another person, especially that of a woman. Would Diane enjoy having all her own way? Jeanette wondered, watching her eyes light with a sort of teasing triumph as Craig agreed to go for a walk. But Jeanette felt certain Craig's indulgence was only temporary; most likely he pandered to Diane on account of what she had so recently suffered. Jeanette just couldn't see him as the manageable, pliant type of husband; on the contrary, having had experience of his dominating and coercive moods, she could imagine his wife having to resign herself, from the very first, to his absolute authority.

They had to step out briskly, because of the cold, and although Jeanette was enjoying the walk she soon discovered, much to her dismay, that this was to be one of those rare instances when she was to have trouble with her leg. They had not proceeded far when she began to limp. Craig noticed it immediately, and said at once that they must turn back. Diane, deep in conversation with Mark, did not at first understand the reason for Craig's decision and offered another objection.

'Jeanette can't go on,' Craig said firmly, and after a small hesitation, 'Look, there's no need for you two to come back, if you're enjoying your walk. I'll go back with Jeanette.'

For a brief moment Jeanette stared at him in wonder-

141

ment, surprised by his offer. Didn't he mind leaving Diane? Then the explanation became clear. He probably did mind, very much, but Jeanette was his guest – and Craig was a stickler for etiquette.

'Are you sure you don't want us all to come back?' Diane asked, trying to peer at Jeanette in the darkness.

'No, you certainly mustn't come back – but I'm an awful nuisance,' she apologized, feeling she should offer to go back alone, or ask Mark to accompany her. 'I've spoilt it for everyone.'

'Nonsense,' Craig put in, rather curtly. 'I wasn't at all enthusiastic about walking in the first place, so it's no hardship for me to return home with you.'

Mark was clearly anxious, but Diane, in her usual impulsive and friendly fashion, had already slipped an arm through his as if taking for granted his willingness to continue the walk with her.

'Come on, then, Mark. Let Craig take Jeanette back.'

'We won't be long,' Mark promised. 'And if you don't feel any better after the rest I'll go round and fetch the car to take you home from Craig's.'

'There's no need, Mark. I can run you both home in mine.'

'I'm so sorry, Craig,' murmured Jeanette as they left Diane and Mark. 'It hasn't troubled me for ages; it would have to start now.'

'My dear girl,' he returned with some asperity, 'I've already said it's no hardship for me to turn back with you. Please don't let me have to repeat it again.'

She fell silent then, the impatience in his voice convincing her more than ever that she was causing him trouble and inconvenience.

'Does it hurt?' he asked after a while. 'You seem to be limping pretty badly now.'

'No, it doesn't hurt too much. It's a sort of dull ache, but the doctor said it would be like this. In another month or so I'll not be feeling any pain at all.' Inevitably he must be thinking again of her wilful disregard of his advice, thinking that she more than deserved all that had come to her.

Fortunately, they hadn't gone far, so they soon reached the house again. On entering the sitting-room they were met with the pungent smell of wood burning as the juniper logs crackled and glowed in the hearth, shooting tiny points of fire up the wide, brass-cowled chimney. The only other illumination was the soft and muted light from a small table lamp away in a corner. Craig's hand went up to the main switch, then fell to his side again as he followed Jeanette into the room.

'On there,' he said abruptly, indicating the couch. 'Put your feet up.'

Some unfinished knitting lay on the couch; Mrs. Fleming's, evidently, and one glance revealed that she had come to the end of her wool.

'Your mother is sitting there,' Jeanette said, making for a chair. 'I think she's gone for some more wool.'

Craig was by the fire and he turned, a log of wood in his hand.

'Move it,' he said. 'Mother can sit somewhere else.' He threw the log on the fire and picked up another.

'I'll be all right on the chair.' Jeanette sat down, reluctant to vex his mother by taking her place.

Impatiently Craig put down the log and proceeded to move the knitting.

'On here,' he ordered, and then, almost glowering at her, 'Why must we always have these arguments?'

'Your mother might not like—'

'Jeanette,' he said darkly, advancing purposefully towards her, 'get on to that couch before I put you there myself!'

She obeyed with as much speed as her leg would allow; Craig slipped off her shoes and she sat propped against the cushions, her legs stretched out, feeling unaccountably helpless, and savouring the exquisite pain of his attention while at the same time relaxing, content to be managed. He leant over her, his dark eyes kindling.

143

'This is the result of your foolhardy determination to ignore any advice I may consider it necessary to give. I told you not to go with Rustem.'

Advice? It had been an order, and, piqued by it, she decided there and then to set his will at defiance, to let him see that she would do exactly as she pleased. How galling now to be forced to own to his wisdom, to have to lie here unable to utter a word in defence of her action. Strangely, though, she felt no resentment; on the contrary, his kindling glance made her feel miserable and in an effort to draw him out of this forbidding mood she admitted that she had made a mistake in not taking notice of what he said. This, however, did not have the desired effect, for he went on to say, with unchanged severity and impatience of tone, that it was always the same whenever he proffered her advice or told her what to do.

'Oh, no, Craig, not always—'

'Look at you just now. What was the sense of standing there arguing about where you should sit?' Automatically, he brought her forward to move a cushion into a more comfortable position; she lay back again, staring up in wonderment at his action. 'I might as well tell you that if I'd had to put you here myself you'd have gone across my knee first! – for I've just about come to the end of my. . . .' He tailed off, aware of his mother's tall and austere figure in the doorway. Jeanette flushed hotly, wondering how long she had been there, and how much she had heard.

It seemed an eternity before the silence was broken. Mrs. Fleming appeared to be incapable of movement, and continued to stand there, in the doorway, her eyes narrowed, a flush spreading across her arrogant face, a flush which Jeanette felt certain stemmed from anger. Jeanette herself had never experienced greater discomfort and embarrassment, but Craig was totally calm and self-possessed as he waited for his mother to speak.

There was a sudden snap and the room was flooded

with light. Mrs. Fleming came forward, mechanically twisting the ball of wool in her fingers, her eyes moving slowly from Craig to Jeanette, and then back again to her son.

'Something wrong, Craig? Is Jeanette ill?'

Jeanette's flush deepened; she was being deliberately ignored by Craig's mother, whose back was now turned towards her.

Craig noticed the slight; his eyes glinted like steel and his voice had a coldly metallic ring as he explained why he and Jeanette had turned back so soon after starting out on their walk.

'Mark and Diane have gone on for a while,' he added. 'There was no need for them to return. They were enjoying the walk.'

'But surely it was Mark's place to look after his sister?'

A frightening little silence followed. Clearly Craig was having difficulty with his temper, for two little white patches had appeared at the corners of his mouth. However, when he spoke his voice was low and controlled, and Jeanette guessed that she was seeing an example of the diplomacy which her brother had mentioned yesterday when they were talking about Craig and his mother.

'There's nothing seriously wrong with Jeanette, so it was quite unnecessary for Mark to turn back. As I've said, he and Diane were enjoying their walk.'

'Didn't Diane mind being deserted like that?'

'Deserted?' An arrogant lift of Craig's brows supported the question. 'I don't quite understand you, Mother. I left Diane in Mark's company.'

It was Mrs. Fleming's turn to suffer embarrassment; she half turned to throw Jeanette a glance of aversion as if considering her entirely to blame for her own uncomfortable position.

Jeanette's face was pale now; she looked up solemnly at Craig and murmured, apologetically,

'I feel much better. I think I would like to walk along

and meet the others. They should be on their way back by now.' She sat up, looking about for her shoes. Craig told her to stay where she was.

'I'll run you home just as soon as Mark gets back. And if I were you I should go straight to bed. That leg of yours needs rest.' Catching her eye, he gave her a faintly mocking smile. No need to wonder at his thoughts.

'Yes, I shall go straight to bed,' and she cast him a glance, from under her lashes, which clearly said, 'in spite of what you're thinking.'

His smile broadened, but retained its hint of mockery. Jeanette waited for the sarcastic rejoinder which was clearly on his lips, but he was suddenly aware of his mother's cold yet interested stare and he merely said, abruptly,

'Sensible girl, the rest will do you good.' And then, saying he would go and bring the car round to the front door, he left the room.

Mrs. Fleming lifted up her knitting from the chair where Craig had put it, and sat down.

'Forgive me, my dear, if I seemed taken aback when I came in,' she said, picking up the two ends of her wool and preparing to join them. 'It was such an odd sort of conversation to be taking place between – mere acquaintances.'

Acquaintances? More like well-sworn enemies, half the time! and as for a conversation . . . no conversation at all, reflected Jeanette, flushing at the memory of the angry threat to which Mrs. Fleming alluded; her son had done all the talking.

'Craig was only – only teasing me,' she stammered rather lamely, recalling that there had been nothing in the least teasing in Craig's manner; on the contrary, he looked as if nothing would have given him greater satisfaction than to carry out his threat – right there and then.

'I should hope he was,' Mrs. Fleming returned, 'though he certainly didn't sound as if he were. I would never have suspected Craig of such frivolity. I think the sooner he is married and settled down the better. He's been on his own far too long.'

Jeanette swallowed a hard little lump in her throat and could find nothing to say to that. Mrs. Fleming fell silent, too, becoming involved with her pattern. But after a while she spoke again, coolly, and without any apparent interest.

'Mark was telling me, at dinner, that you received your injury in a climbing accident.'

'Yes, I did.' Jeanette sat up and reached for her shoes.

'You've done some climbing before?'

'That was the first time.'

'How very unfortunate – for you to have an accident on your first venture.' Mrs. Fleming joined her wool and let the ball roll on to the floor. 'Did you not have an experienced person with you?'

'We did, yes – and he shouted a warning, but I didn't know what he meant.' Jeanette cocked an ear, listening for the car. How long would Craig be? she wondered, anxious to bring this polite conversation to an end.

'So it was a properly organized expedition?' Mrs. Fleming raised her eyes from her work. Jeanette frowned slightly, puzzled.

'Certainly it was. Our leader, a young Turk, is the son of a famous climber.'

'So it was a mixed party? Your brother didn't say, but I did wonder.' She held up her work, apparently absorbed in the pattern. Jeanette's frown deepened. Where was this leading? 'Tell me, my dear, what happens on a trip like that? Obviously it takes several days. Do you stay in hotels, or climbing huts ... or what?'

Silence. Jeanette slipped her feet into her shoes and then straightened up.

'We slept in the open, Mrs. Fleming, in sleeping bags.'

The knitting was lowered slowly on to Mrs. Fleming's knee. She turned to regard her companion in rather mild astonishment for a space and then, with a shrug and the

147

merest shake of her head, she remarked that she must be getting old, for she failed to understand the ways of modern youth, and Jeanette was reminded of that other occasion when this woman had made a similar subtle thrust, hinting on the impropriety of her staying at the *yali* with her son. But this time her insinuations were more pointed, probably because her son was not involved, Jeanette concluded, and Mrs. Fleming's next words supported this idea.

'I know that sort of thing is accepted nowadays, but I must confess I'm glad that Craig is older – and a stickler for the proprieties.'

Jeanette's eyes flashed; she was about to ask what was meant by 'that sort of thing' when she pulled herself up, quelling her anger. She was Craig's guest; he mustn't come in and find her quarrelling with his mother. But Mrs. Fleming's next words made it more difficult than ever for Jeanette to maintain her calm, for she expressed surprise that Mark had countenanced the trip, adding that Craig would never have done so, had Jeanette been a sister of his.

'I think I told you once before, Mrs. Fleming, that my brother wouldn't presume to interfere in my actions.' She ignored the reference to Craig, but something in his mother's manner convinced Jeanette that she was curious to know whether her son was aware of the fact that they had all slept out in the open, and that she was manoeuvring the conversation into channels where the question could be asked without appearing too outrageous. Jeanette waited, debating on her reply, but the question did not come. Mrs. Fleming seemed to realize that so bald an inquiry could not be put to Jeanette herself . . . but Jeanette was sure it would later be put to her son.

Quietness reigned for a while, with the older woman becoming absorbed in her work and Jeanette watching the window for the headlights of the car, while at the same time listening for the return of Mark and Diane.

They all came in together, Craig having parked the car

at the front door just as the other two came up the drive.

'All right?' Mark smiled, without evincing much concern, and it was apparent that Craig had assured him that she was now free from pain. Mark turned to his friend. 'It's good of you to run us home, Craig. I could have gone and fetched the car, you know.'

Craig shrugged that off and, taking Jeanette's coat from the back of the chair where he had placed it when they came in, held it out for her to put on.

'Thank you, Craig.' She smiled up at him, aware of his mother's narrowed gaze, and also aware of the strange and flickering glance that passed from Diane to Craig. Jeanette felt her colour rise. Could it be that Diane was displeased by this little attention which her future husband extended to another woman? Surely not, for wasn't it Diane herself who had encouraged Craig to walk back home with her? Yet Craig's glance, too, was strange, as he looked back at Diane. Was he apologizing? – trying to explain that, as Jeanette was his guest, he had a certain duty towards her?

Jeanette's shoulders sagged; the pleasure she had derived from having Craig's sole attention, brief though it was, became crushed under the weight of misery that now engulfed her.

Craig was merely performing a duty, had been doing so from the moment he realized he would have to bring her back home. And now he was apologizing to Diane who was – perhaps understandably – annoyed.

But as she and Mark preceded Craig out to the car Jeanette saw the smile that Diane suddenly bestowed on him, a smile that promised a wonderful making up, later, when they could find themselves alone.

Mrs. Fleming and Diane left Istanbul at the end of the week. On the evening before their departure they had dined with Mark and Jeanette, Tony having accepted a previous invitation to visit some friends. Jeanette would have liked to make some excuse to go out, but she could

149

not let Mark down and she resigned herself to another evening of strain. Craig on this occasion was more attentive than ever to Diane and it was plain that he hated the idea of the coming parting even though it would, this time, be only temporary.

Mrs. Fleming's satisfaction was unmistakable; she watched Diane and Craig all the while, just as she had on the evening when they had all dined at the Hilton, and, forgetting all her usual decorum, she turned impulsively to Jeanette and said,

'It's good to see my son so happy. I have waited a long time for this.'

Mark's eyes had met those of his sister, in that sort of comforting way which was becoming more and more mystifying as time went on.

When they were leaving Craig fetched Diane's wrap, and as he held it out she turned so that he could put it round her.

'Thanks, darling.' She twisted her head to smile. Craig's hands remained on her shoulders, holding her close to him. With an almost imperceptive movement Craig's head came down and his lips touched Diane's hair. Jeanette looked away, pressing her fingers against the sudden stab of pain in her temple.

'Be careful, dear,' said Craig a few minutes later when, going down the steps, Diane appeared to stumble. 'Give me your hand.'

Mark and Jeanette walked down with them to the end of the garden where they all stood for a few more minutes, talking. The Bosphorus, turbulent from the cross-currents coming down from the Black Sea, seemed to match Jeanette's mood to perfection. Never had she been so restless, so gripped by tumult. And for the next few weeks she threw herself once more into the gay and aimless round. There were parties in the little wooden cafés on the shores of the strait; there were dinners and dances and night clubs, both the fashionable kind and those to which a man never takes his wife.

But this kind of night life was exhausting, and by the middle of October she was spent. Moreover, it was all so futile; she could never forget Craig while she lived so near.

It had been arranged that she should move in with Sally and Gwen when her brother's term at the university expired, but now Jeanette had practically decided to return to England with Mark at Christmas.

She mentioned this to him one Sunday afternoon when they were alone. He lowered his book on to his lap and cast her a sidelong glance.

'It would mean breaking your contract.'

'Yes, I've thought about that, Mark, and I know it isn't the right thing to do.' She stared at him broodingly, wondering at the strangeness of his expression.

'It would go on your report,' he warned. 'And it would go against you if you ever applied for a job abroad again.'

'I'm not contemplating working abroad again, so it wouldn't matter very much if it did go on my report.' Strange, she thought, that he hadn't inquired as to the reason for this sudden decision to return to England after what would be only two terms at the school. There was again that hint of compassion in his eyes, that pity and concern she had first encountered on the day of the climbing accident, and on so many occasions since.

He spoke at last, in tones edged with regret.

'When I asked you to come out here I thought it was for the best, that it would help you to forget that other misfortune; instead, you've—' He broke off, realizing his slip. Jeanette stared, once again recalling the day of the accident.

'Mark. . . .'

'Yes?'

'When I was under the influence of the drugs – when I was rambling – what did I say?'

He looked thoughtfully at her, undecided for a while.

'You talked about Craig,' he told her slowly at last, and her colour heightened.

'What did I say?'

Again he hesitated, and then,

'Enough,' he answered briefly.

She looked past him, unseeingly, to the dark outline of a clump of cypress trees away on a distant ridge.

'So . . . you know?' She brought her gaze back to stare at him bleakly. 'I wondered at the time what I'd been saying – I felt it was something that had upset you, but I didn't think I'd have talked about – about Craig.'

They both turned as, unobtrusively, Metat entered the room with the tea-tray. He drew forth a small table and set the tray upon it. Then, silently, he went out, closing the door behind him. Jeanette poured the tea and they sat in silence for a while, neither seeming willing to voice their thoughts. But at last Mark spoke regretfully of having asked her to come over to Turkey, saying again that he'd thought, at the time, that it would help her to forget the past.

'You don't know how I feel,' he went on, in tones of deep concern. 'It never entered my head that you might – that Craig would appeal to you – damn it, Jeanette, how did it happen? You knew, dear, from the first, about Diane.'

How did it happen? Again she glanced bleakly at him . . . and suddenly she was astounded by his expression. His face was grey, almost as if he were suffering just as much as she. He mustn't be troubled like this, must not feel so guilty and unhappy on her account.

'It will pass,' she said lightly, smiling as she picked up the cake-stand and held it out to him. 'It isn't anything – anything deep, because, as you say, I've always known about Diane.' She gave a little laugh, hoping he hadn't noticed how broken it sounded. 'He's rather attractive, and it was nice being escorted by him, but it's – it's only infatuation—'

'Stop it, Jeanette. You're not convincing either yourself or me.' He waved aside her offer of the cakes, and she put down the stand abruptly. 'Why, for heaven's sake, did you go to the island? That was only adding to your misery, surely?'

'I explained, Mark, that I really had no alternative. Don't worry, it didn't hurt. ...' What was the use? To her consternation her eyes filled up and despite her efforts at control the tears rolled unchecked down her face. She found a handkerchief and dried her eyes, while Mark watched her, his own eyes dark with anxiety and remorse.

'If only I'd thought – used my sense—'

'Don't blame yourself; you mustn't. No one can foresee these things, Mark. They just happen and no one can help it.' She looked steadfastly into her brother's dark, handsome face ... and wondered at his expression. It was unfathomable; his gaze was distant, his lips tight and hard and for a moment he reminded her of Craig at his most austere.

'They just happen. ...' He spoke to himself, forgetting her presence. 'Yes, they just happen and no one can help it.'

CHAPTER TEN

VERY little was seen of Craig for several weeks following the departure of his mother and Diane, for he spent every week-end at the *yali*, and although he attended the usual round of Consulate functions with Mark and Tony, his evenings were also often taken up with his book. On occasions he would invite Jeanette and the two men to his house for dinner, but Jeanette invariably found an excuse for declining the invitation. At other times he would be Mark's guest, but again she contrived to avoid his company by arranging to go out with her friends. Inevitably they did sometimes meet, but Craig had now adopted that air of cool indifference which had characterized his attitude towards her during the first few weeks of their acquaintanceship. In fact, he seemed at times resolved to ignore her presence altogether. If he did speak, it was with a mingling of mockery and contempt. Jeanette accepted all this with pain and resignation, having known from the first that his interest in her must come to an end.

Having learnt from Mark of her determination never to marry, to remain loyal to Ned's memory, Craig had, for some inexplicable reason, set out determinedly to divert her from her chosen path, to draw her out, and away from her aversion to marriage. Having failed in his endeavours, he'd now lost patience – and interest. Perhaps he had at last asked himself why he should bother anyway. His own life was all straightened out and the passage ahead was smooth. Why waste time on a girl who was, as his mother remarked, just an acquaintance? The thought of that brought a quiver to Jeanette's lips. Undoubtedly now, they were drifting into that sort of relationship . . . but they had been more than acquaintances. There had been times, during that unforgettable month on the island, when she and Craig had come very close, when she had felt him to be her true and sincere friend.

And now even his interest was lost.

For this she began to be grateful, much to her surprise. For even the slightest interest bestowed upon her brought a return of that hopeless longing which was always followed by a feeling of utter emptiness and despair.

He should never have interfered in the first place. Had he continued to ignore her, to treat her with that initial indifference, she would never have begun to care. It was his sudden and unexpected interest. ... Jeanette pulled herself up. No, Craig Fleming had exerted a forceful and magnetic influence on her from the moment she had set eyes on him. Hadn't she bitterly resented that influence? – made a determined effort to dislike him, blaming him for the guilt she experienced at the knowledge that she was gradually recovering from the pain of losing Ned?

No, much as she would like to blame Craig for this heartache, in all fairness she found herself quite unable to do so.

One evening Mark mentioned that Craig was coming over later and would stay to supper.

'Do you mind if I go out?' she asked apologetically, feeling guilty at these repeated excuses. 'I don't want to be here when he comes.'

'No, dear, you go.' He paused. 'Anything special in view?'

'There's a party at the flat – fancy dress. I said I wouldn't go....'

'You'll enjoy it, surely?' He seemed concerned and Jeanette gave him a rather wan little smile.

'They're a nice enough crowd, only....'

'Yes?'

'They become rather rowdy after a while.'

'Too much to drink?' he queried, and she nodded her head.

'I'd rather go there than meet Craig, though.' She hesitated. 'I'll be glad to be home, Mark.'

'So will I. It won't be long. What did they say when

you handed in your resignation?'

'They weren't pleased.' She gave a little grimace.

'It certainly isn't the done thing to break one's contract. As you said, I'm finished as regards getting a post abroad again.'

'Pity. You might just want to after a while. Still, it's done now. They did accept your resignation, though?'

'I shall know in a few days' time, after the meeting. But I did emphasize my determination to leave at Christmas.' No use carrying on in this way. While ever she remained in Istanbul she would never be able to forget Craig.

Having declined the invitation, Jeanette naturally had nothing to wear. This troubled her for a while and then, remembering that there were several fancy dress costumes at the flat, she felt sure one of her friends would be willing to lend her something.

'Is someone coming for you?' Mark glanced at the clock. 'Or do you want me to take you?'

'If you don't mind, Mark. Could you?' He looked tired, she thought, remembering that the *odos* had blown up again, and wondering if he was feeling the effects of it.

'Certainly,' he assented, smiling. 'What about coming home?'

'I don't know. I haven't arranged anything.' Sally would willingly run her home, she knew. But Çetin would be there, and should he offer her a lift she could not very well refuse without offering her friends some explanation. 'If you could manage to fetch me?'

'Of course. What time?'

'Oh—' She shrugged. 'I should say about twelve. I don't expect the party will be breaking up by then, but it's late enough for you to be coming out.'

'You're sure? I'll come any time you like.'

'I'm sure, Mark. I shall have had enough by then.' The dejection in her voice troubled him and he said gently,

'Stay in if you prefer it, Jeanette. Craig isn't coming until about nine; and you could make an excuse and go to bed immediately after supper.'

She shook her head emphatically.

'No, I'd rather go.'

Sally and Gwen were delighted that Jeanette had changed her mind, and Sally immediately set about finding her something to wear.

'I've lent out several costumes, and haven't had them back, but there's all this filmy draping. You won't object to being a slave of the harem, will you?' she said with a grin.

'What will I wear underneath?' Jeanette regarded with acute distaste the filmy length of cloth. It was so transparent it would provide scarcely any covering at all. 'Have you nothing else I can wear?'

'This will be all right. You can wear my bikini underneath. You'll look fine!'

Jeanette shook her head. She felt ready to go home, but she could hardly ask Sally to take her back when the guests were even now beginning to arrive.

Gwen dashed into the bedroom.

'How goes it? You should see Mustafa – he's come as the Sultan; he looks fabulous!'

'Jeanette's not very thrilled with being Mustafa's slave,' Sally returned with a laugh. 'Don't you think she'll look great with this over my bikini?'

'Just right. Teresa's come as a slave of the harem, and she's got a filmy thing like that over a bikini.' She glanced down at her own dress; she was in the Turkish peasant costume. 'Wish I'd thought of it myself – though I rather fancied this. Do come on, you two,' she added. 'The Grand Vizir's pouring drinks.'

'Who's the Grand Vizir?'

'Çetin. He looks great!'

There seemed nothing for it but to wear the bikini and the tulle, and a little while later Jeanette, complete with yashmak, emerged from the bedroom and joined the gay, gaudily-attired throng in the sitting-room.

Several others arrived dressed as ladies of the harem, and two young men came as Sultans, to Mustafa's great disgust. There weren't enough slaves, he grumbled.

'How are we to share them out? I thought I was to have five all to myself!'

Soon the party was in full swing. As the men were requested to bring a bottle of wine as their entrance 'fee' there was plenty of drink to go round. Jeanette had never acquired the taste for Turkish wines and no amount of persuasion would tempt her to take any now.

Gary, a young representative for one of the oil companies, fetched her an iced lemonade and stood talking to her while they watched two of the girls trying unsuccessfully to perform a belly dance.

By eleven-thirty the party was becoming rather wild, and Sally, her face flushed with anger, came and sat beside Jeanette.

'Isn't it awful! It's those people Çetin's brought; I've never set eyes on them before tonight.' They were mostly English; two of the men who had had more than enough to drink were singing loudly, holding their glasses aloft. A couple were sitting on the couch, locked in each other's arms, oblivious of everyone around them, and in the tiny space in the middle of the floor two other couples were vainly trying to keep time to the music blaring forth from the record player in the corner. 'It's bedlam,' Sally went on, 'but it won't happen again. I hate a party to get this way. Çetin has no right to bring people like that.'

Gwen came up, and she, too, was angry at the way these strangers were behaving. Jeanette, most unhappy herself, felt intensely sorry for her friends, agreeing that Çetin should have known better than to bring people of this type to the flat.

'Can't we stop them singing? It sounds so vulgar.' Gwen twisted her head, looking for Çetin. 'I'm going to tell him to take them off.'

But Çetin was at the 'bar' and Gwen could not attract his attention. She rose to go to him. It was now a quarter to twelve and Jeanette also got up, saying she would change her clothes.

'Mark's coming for me at twelve,' she reminded them. 'Is it all right for me to use the bedroom?'

'Of course; help yourself. . . .' Sally tailed off, her eyes taking on an almost horrified expression and Jeanette turned swiftly to discover the cause of this. Her own eyes dilated and she felt herself actually trembling. For, standing in the doorway, his gaze travelling slowly round the room, searching for her, was Craig. Gwen and Sally were clearly put out; they both flushed hotly and Sally rose and turned off the record player. The couples stopped dancing and silence descended as every eye was turned on Craig.

'I did ring, but no one heard.' His eyes flicked Jeanette; she squirmed under their icy contempt. 'Mark had a headache, so I offered to come instead.' His voice was a whiplash, and his eyes travelled slowly from her head to her feet. She felt naked and almost sick with mortification as the colour fused her cheeks and spread right up to her temples. 'I expect you have a coat?'

'I – yes—' Slowly she came out of her stupor. 'I'll go and change – if – if you don't mind waiting?'

'Do sit down, Mr. Fleming,' she heard Gwen say as, turning, she almost ran into the bedroom.

He was in the tiny hall when she came out; she merely called good night and followed him downstairs and out to the car.

The silence was awful and for a while Jeanette continued to writhe under the censure and disdain it implied. But then her anger rose. Why should she be affected in this way by his opinion of her? He meant nothing to her and his approval or disapproval was of no account. He had no right at all to take it upon himself to adopt this censorious attitude. He had elected to come for her and the circumstances in which he had found her were none of his business.

She leant back, determined to quell this feeling of shame, but it was no use. She was too intensely aware of his contempt; the strength of it seemed to fill the car. Impatient and angry he had often been, but never had he treated her to so scornful a silence as this. Her eyelids pricked as she recalled that wonderful sense of companionship which had come to them as they stood in the Palace of Topkapi, and which had gained in strength during the idyllic month on Büyük Ada. Her wretchedness increased as she realized that his disdain must naturally extend to Sally and Gwen. That he could hold them in contempt troubled her and on impulse she made an effort to dispel the impression he must now have of them.

'Craig, I don't know what you're thinking of – of Sally and Gwen, but please don't imagine their parties are always like that.' He drove on in silence and she added, painfully, 'They do sometimes become rowdy, I admit, but what you saw tonight was not typical.' Still no response. Craig continued to look straight ahead, his strong brown fingers merely resting on the wheel. 'It – it m-must have seemed – awful. ...' She tailed off, mortified that she should be stammering.

They travelled quickly along the almost deserted Necati Bey Caddesi, leaving behind the lights of the old city and the wide outer harbour of the Golden Horn, still alive with fishing boats, their lanterns bobbing about, sprinkling the water with light. They passed the Dolmabaçhe and Çeragan Palaces, traversed the Çeragan Caddesi and still the almost frightening silence continued. They would soon be home; she sensed his intention of dropping her off at the door and driving away without even a word. She couldn't let him leave like this, despising her friends.

'Please, Craig, don't get the wrong impression. Some people came whom Sally and Gwen didn't know of. If it hadn't been for them there would have been no – vulgarity.'

She heard a smothered exclamation of surprise, and Craig took his foot off the accelerator for a second.

'You don't consider your own get-up, then, to have

been vulgar?'

Jeanette began to say why she had come to wear the costume, and then stopped, angry that she should be almost eagerly pouring forth explanations when she ought to be telling him in no uncertain terms to mind his own business. She ended up by adding, defiantly,

'My costume suited the occasion!'

'You're quite right, it did,' he agreed, and she bit her lip in vexation at providing him an opening like that. 'Does Mark know what goes on there?'

'What do you mean by that?' She sat up straight, flushing with anger.

'Don't be naïve – And this indignation is out of place after what I've seen tonight.' The merest pause, and then, 'I noticed your young Turkish friend was there. Did you dance with him in that get-up?'

'Please don't keep calling it a get-up,' she flashed. 'No, I didn't dance with Çetin,' she added, and sensed the sceptical lift of his brows in the darkness. His foot came down on the accelerator again and the buildings and the park and the shadowy outlines of the tall cypress trees flashed past as the car purred forward with smoothly-increasing speed. Craig spoke softly, ignoring her protest.

'Rustem obviously has some excuse for his amorous approaches. I'm amazed that you took exception on one particular occasion. I knew, in spite of your protests to the contrary, that there must have been some preliminaries to the little exhibition I interrupted.' His attention was on his driving as they caught up with, and passed, a slower car. 'Perhaps I should apologize for that? I imagined I was doing you a service – but I now strongly suspect I was mistaken.'

A gasp of fury caught at her throat, preventing speech. If he hadn't been at the wheel of the car she was sure she'd have lost control and slapped his face. She bitterly regretted opening the conversation, for he was clearly unprepared to listen to her attempts to rectify the im-

pression he'd inevitably gained of Sally and Gwen. She
sought for some biting and equally hurtful retort to his
hateful implications, but the anger in her throat still held
her speechless, and even when, eventually, she managed
to articulate her words all she could find to say was a
trite and rather half-hearted,

'How dare you speak to me like this!'

'Don't be ridiculous.' He spoke quietly, too quietly, she
thought, trying to shake off an odd sense of danger that
was slowly creeping over her. It amazed her to discover
that, in a vague sort of way, she was wishing he would
lose his temper. 'I find you, indecently dressed, in company that can only be described as undesirable, and you
adopt this attitude of indignation, regarding my plain
speaking as an affront.'

'Not an affront, an insult!'

To her surprise he flung back his head and laughed, a
hateful, derisive laugh that not only served to increase
her misgivings, but also made him a stranger to her.
Craig, possessing as he did that air of cool detachment
which seemed to lift him above a display of emotion –
Craig, to laugh like that. Çetin it would have suited, but
it seemed altogether alien to Craig's character.

A prolonged silence followed and was broken only
when they had turned into the drive and the car was
brought to a standstill.

'It looks as if Mark's in bed.' Jeanette spoke stiffly,
not wishing to speak at all but impelled to break the
silence, for, in some unfathomable way, it troubled her.
'Did he say he intended doing so?'

'I advised him to. I suspect it's the *odos* again.'
Reaching across, he opened the door, then he slid from
the car and waited until she came round to join him.
The house was in darkness except for a shade of light
visible through the curtains in the sitting-room.

'Thank you for bringing me home.' She looked up at
Craig, her lips trembling. It was so ridiculous to be hurt,
to be sunk in misery because of his contempt. His opinion

could not affect her in the least; quite soon she would be back in England and it was most unlikely that she would ever set eyes on him again. 'I'll be all right now. I expect Mark will have left the door, but in any case, I have a key.'

'I'll come in with you.' he said quietly, and her eyes flew to his, searching in the darkness for some sign that would explain the reason for her increasing uneasiness.

He followed her into the sitting-room. How quiet he was. Where was the impatience, the anger he always meted out whenever she did anything of which he didn't approve? One light only had been left on, the small table lamp in the corner. The fire had practically died, but the air still hung with that heady, seductive scent of smouldering juniper logs.

'I wonder if Metat is still up?' The murmured words came automatically, as if in response to some inner fear. Why this feeling of insecurity? Whatever mood Craig had been in, she had always felt safe with him. She took off her coat, hoping the prosaic action would restore her common sense. It was so ridiculous to be this way, with her heartbeats increasing all the time, and a little ball of fear gathering in her throat. She placed her coat over the back of a chair and looked at Craig. He stood by the cabinet, holding one of the little votive offerings in his hand, but his eyes were on Jeanette, dark and penetrating.

'Metat and Mrs. Baydur retired before I came out to fetch you,' he told her, and returning the crude clay figure to its place, he came slowly towards her. She tilted her head, attracted yet repelled by his cold, unemotional features. They might have been etched in stone.

'Mrs. Baydur, too?' She was seeking for words. Why didn't he go?

'Mrs. Baydur, too,' he echoed, a hint of mocking amusement entering his voice. 'Were you wanting her for something?'

'No.' She shook her head vigorously, realizing with a sense of shock that she was deriving great comfort from the knowledge of Mark's being in the bedroom above. 'It's time I went up. It's quite late. . . .' She waited for him to take the hint, but he still stood there, looking down at her. 'Thank you again for bringing me home.'

'Telling me to go?' The lift of his eyebrows conveyed rebuke, though his voice retained its hint of amusement. 'That's not very hospitable of you, Jeanette.'

She darted him a glance of surprise, she had thought his every mood was known to her, but Craig in this vein was a total stranger. Unconsciously she extended her hands in a little gesture of bewilderment.

'I don't understand you at all tonight—'

'No? Well, perhaps you'll understand this better.' His hands shot out and gripped her wrists and the next instant she was struggling in his arms.

'Craig, how can you!' She was stunned by his action. Her thoughts flew to Diane and she added in a trembling suffocated voice, 'You must be drunk!'

'Drunk, am I?' Strangely he took no exception to that. One arm slackened its brutal hold; his hand came up to caress her cheek, before he slid his fingers through her hair, drawing it away from her face and holding it lingeringly for a moment. Then Jeanette uttered a sharp cry of pain and protest as her head was unceremoniously jerked back. Her heart thumped madly against him. Surely he must feel it, she thought, despairing at the futility of her struggles. She tried to move her head in order to escape his compelling gaze, but the effort merely produced another cry of pain, and she was forced to meet his eyes. No coldness now in their depths, or in the dark face so close above her own.

'Drunk, am I?' he said again. 'Must I be drunk before I become flesh and blood?'

She gasped at that and her thoughts darted to Çetin and the night of Craig's timely arrival on the scene.

'Let me go! I'll call my brother – I don't care if you are his friend!'

'Call away,' he said, amused, and, when her eyes

flickered uncomprehendingly, 'Mark, I hope, is sleeping soundly under the influence of my famous cure.'

Of course. She should have guessed. If Mark were suffering from the effects of the *odos* it would be quite natural for Craig to dose him with the draught he had once given her. Her consternation grew as she recalled how soundly she had slept. Mark would be dead to everything until lunch time tomorrow. No use calling for the servants, either, for they slept in the annexe at the far end of the house. Craig read her thoughts and his amusement grew.

'No escape for you, is there, my dear? Had I deliberately planned the situation it couldn't have succeeded better—'

'I believe you did plan it!' The words were uttered before she had given herself time to think. 'I have no idea why you're suddenly treating me like this, but. . . .' With a sudden flash of insight she knew the cause of those vague and increasing fears she had begun to experience on the way home in the car. That calm control was alien to Craig's nature; it was that unaccustomed restraint that had troubled her, for she knew she was coming off far too lightly. Subconsciously she had been awaiting the explosion, steeling her nerves for the cutting reprimands that must inevitably be delivered. But this reaction staggered her, being equally as uncharacteristic as his previous calm acceptance – or what appeared to be his calm acceptance – of what he had seen at the flat.

'Planned?'

'I'm sorry. You couldn't have known you'd be coming to fetch me home.' She tried to free her hands, to press them to her aching head, but they were effectively imprisoned against the hardness of his chest.

'Nor had any idea of the state of undress in which I would find you,' he commented, and without giving her the chance of thinking up an answer to that he went on, 'As for my treatment of you – I think, if you're honest, you will agree that you've been asking for it for some time, keeping me at arm's length with your own particular brand of defence.' He released her hair, sliding his arm down to encircle her waist. 'But it wasn't like that with Çetin, was it? You never put on your armour with him, did you?'

'I don't know what you mean, keeping you at arm's length.' The most staggering idea flashed through her bewildered brain as she recalled several occasions when Craig had been so close, so in harmony with her that it seemed impossible to think of him merely as a friend. Had he had other ideas? He had been on his own for a long time, leading a life made unnatural by the fact of his having to wait for another man's wife. But he was a man for all that, with all the normal needs and desires of a healthy vigorous male. Jeanette recalled too his indifference during her first month in Turkey ... and then his sudden interest – and it had been sudden, taking her completely by surprise. Then there had been the time when he had angrily told her she ought to take what life had to offer. On that occasion they had been talking about the Sultan's sons. ... Yes, Jeanette understood now. Craig's interest had always puzzled her, chiefly because she knew that Diane was his one and only love.

But he wasn't averse to finding consolation until the time when she could come to him.

Sickened by the sudden revelation, Jeanette wondered how many women, during the past fifteen years, had succumbed to his persuasive powers – and to his charms. She suspected there had been many. Hadn't Craig's mother said that she, Jeanette, 'would not be the first to lose her heart'?

No wonder he had so often shown anger and impatience. Jeanette understood the reason for those outbursts now. And on a couple of occasions his frustration had reached the point where he had actually threatened her with violence. He knew, from Mark, that she'd come out to Turkey to forget a sorrow, and he probably thought that she was what men termed 'easy game'. How galling for him to meet with a rebuff each time he made an advance! Jeanette could imagine just how much his pride had suffered during these past few months.

His arms suddenly tightened and she was caught in a merciless grip that jerked her back to the present and to the awareness of her perilous position. Was she to pay for keeping him at arm's length, as he called it? Did he mean mischief? He certainly looked as though he did for his face in the half light was dark and cruel, and so close that she could almost feel his lips touching hers. Through the mist of her panic she recalled Craig's unnatural control when in the car, and her own vague and inexplicable wish that he would lose his temper. The lash of his tongue she would undoubtedly have felt, but there would have been no physical attack. There were smouldering embers in his eyes now and terror seized her, for this was a new Craig, a man with all his primitive instincts tensed for release.

'I – I never encouraged Çetin—' She could hardly speak for the fear gripping her throat. 'You might think otherwise, but—' The cracked and whispered words were lost in his savage, brutal kisses as his mouth closed remorselessly on hers. Her head, already aching from that cruel grip on her hair, began to throb as if in sympathy with the quivering nerves of her body.

Craig was trying to enforce from her some response and she deliberately stiffened, returning nothing either with her body or her lips. He would derive scant satisfaction from kissing and embracing a lifeless log. But he was aware of her resistance; it infuriated him and she suffered for it. Her whole frame felt crushed and bruised when at last he relaxed his hold and held her away from him.

'No reciprocation?' he said harshly, his fingers eating into her waist. 'I'll wager that's not how you react to your young Turkish friend!'

'I think you must be mad!' Jeanette put up a trembling hand to her mouth, as if to feel the bruises there. Her struggles began again, born of fear, but his fingers

167

tightened even more viciously and she ceased abruptly, stemming the cry of pain that rose to her lips. 'Çetin has never kissed me like that!'

Too late she realized the unfortunate slip of phrasing; Craig's eyes narrowed and a drift of colour slowly fused his cheeks. His face came close again, dark with fury; his voice was a low and vibrant threat when he spoke.

'How did he kiss you, then?'

'He didn't—' Before she could rectify her mistake his lips were pressed to hers again, with even more brutality than before, and with all the arrogance of primitive possession.

'I daresay it wasn't like that, either!' He looked fit to murder her, though undoubtedly he had something else in mind, and she burst out, desperately and without thought,

'Don't, Craig ... oh, what are you going to do!' Her whole body shuddered against him and she had the rather astounding impression of a gentler hold, and yet his arms about her did not slacken. 'You'll be sorry – Mark—'

His hold did slacken then and to her utter astonishment his black fury dissolved and he actually threw back his head and laughed – a laugh of sheer amusement.

'So that's why you were looking so scared?' His fingers came up and flicked her cheek, caressingly. 'Whatever I would like to do to you – and believe me I would derive the greatest satisfaction from teaching you a lesson – I am your brother's friend. Honour, you know, and all that.' He was mocking her, but although she flushed at his mockery she also experienced a heartfelt relief at this sudden and unexpected change of mood. This was more the Craig she knew and understood. She felt safe again. Nevertheless, her heart did give a jerk as she thought of his words about teaching her a lesson. She felt sure, had she not been Mark's sister, that she would not have come off so lightly. He still held her, though not so closely or so painfully. His dark eyes still retained their mocking light, but there was something else in their depths, something that prompted an effort to regain his esteem.

'Çetin has never kissed me – in any way.' She was still very shaken and her voice reflected·the trembling of her body. 'I suppose you think, after tonight, that I'm – I'm. . . .' She could not continue and the slight lift of Craig's brows was the only response he made to her rather feeble protestations of innocence. 'It really has nothing to do with you, I know, but I would like to think you believed me.' Such humility, when she should be reminding him of his detestable conduct, declaring wrathfully that she hated him. To her dismay her eyes filled up and two great tears rolled slowly down her cheeks. Craig's eyes flickered oddly as he watched her take out a handkerchief and dry her face.

'You can say he's never kissed you? – after that little scene I interrupted – here in this room? And after the Bursa escapade??' His glance was sceptical; Jeanette avoided it, looking past him to the fire, to the faintly glowing embers, shooting out tiny sparks through the bars to fall on to the hearth and die. And then her eyes were drawn irresistibly to the little perfume jar and again she saw Craig handling it, with such care, such reverence almost. She had sensed the strength of his long and slender hands as he held it, and the gentleness with which he examined it before pronouncing his verdict. She had felt that strength a few moments ago, a cruel and merciless strength. She had also felt the gentleness of those hands, but on other occasions . . . not tonight.

An anguished little sigh trembled on her lips as she recalled those moments of intimacy, moments that Craig had forgotten – or perhaps they had never even registered, had been so unimportant as to pass unnoticed.

'About that little scene here, as you call it. I didn't give Çetin any encouragement. On the contrary, I told him I could never marry him—'

'He asked you to marry him?' Craig interrupted sharply, a frown darkening his brow. 'Çetin wanted marriage?'

She nodded and went on perseveringly,

'I told him I couldn't, and he seemed to understand and accept that. I would never have agreed to go out with him otherwise. I felt all the time that he was resigned, and I was amazed when he – acted as he did.'

A small pause and then, curiously,

'He knew you were going out with me?'

'I told him, yes. I'd telephoned him earlier.'

'So he was jealous.'

She flushed but said no more about that, sure now that Craig believed her statement about not giving Çetin any encouragement.

'As regards the Bursa trip. ...' Jeanette shook her head sadly, and with deep regret. 'I should have taken notice of you, Craig, but there was a good reason for my going.'

'Yes?'

'I can't tell you ... it isn't possible.' She looked up at him apologetically, and then continued, 'I know we weren't – I wasn't prudent—'

'Prudent!' he shot out, and she was reminded of his reaction when he heard of the several incidents which had occurred on the trip. He had looked, she remembered, as if he would dearly have loved to do her some physical injury. 'You were downright brazen to sleep out with three men—'

'Craig!'

'You know what I mean,' he snapped, brushing aside her indignant protest. 'And those friends of yours – they don't appear to be over endowed with common sense, either. Why didn't you all book in at a hotel? It wasn't as if you were out in the wilds.'

Jeanette shook her head, unable to answer him, for looking back now it seemed incredible that they had followed like sheep, obeying Çetin's every order without question.

'It was foolish,' she admitted at last, 'but it was only

that. There was no actual wrong intent.' Her tones were pleading, and so were her eyes. It seemed so important that he should think well of her, though she did wonder, with a little catch of depression, whether he would ever forget the way she was dressed tonight. 'I do want you to believe me.' She didn't realize how small and pale she looked, and how distressed. Craig's dark eyes flickered, and settled. He regarded her silently for a while, his face grim and stern but lacking that threatening light which had so terrified her not many moments ago.

'You're the most puzzling and the most tantalizing woman I've ever had the misfortune to meet!' he exploded, almost making her jump, both in surprise and at the unexpected loudness of his tones. 'What sort of warped philosophy has eaten into you? You mustn't marry, yet you can go off with three men to— All right, I'm fully aware that you had two female companions – there's no need to take me quite literally,' he snapped when she would have interrupted him. 'You go off like that – and tonight I find you in the fellow's company again, half undressed, and you adopt this air of virtue, tell me you haven't even been kissed!' He stopped, to glare at her. 'My common sense tells me I ought not to be convinced.'

His outburst staggered her; she gave a little gasp and stared up at him, her face pale and shadowed in the dimness of the room, her lips parted slightly and swollen still by the cruelty of those savage kisses. She shook her head in bewilderment.

'I can never understand you, Craig,' she murmured, wondering if he were convinced, despite his common sense. 'I don't understand anything you do or say when you're like this.' She made a small movement of her hands and continued to stare at him, mystified. 'Why should you bother about me at all? Why should you be so interested in what I do?' Diane intruded and she went on without thinking, 'You and I can never mean anything to one another, because of the past. . . .' She pressed a hand to her mouth, appalled at what she'd said. There had never been any question of anything between them, at least, not in the way implied by her words. What would Craig think? Would he realize she had been speaking her thoughts aloud, and guess at her feelings for him? Fearfully, she cast her eyes upwards, searching for his reaction. What she saw caused her to tremble again and make a move to escape from his arms.

'Very well,' he said between his teeth. 'I'll go, but I'll have another kiss first!'

In total contradiction to the tones of his voice his kisses were gentle, with all the tender persuasion of the lover. Her body went taut and for a while she remained firm in her resolve. But Craig was equally set on her capitulation. She found herself responding and at the same time wondering why she had fought. In their numerous clashes of wills he had always beaten her; physically she could not hope to win.

Her emotions were chaotic. She became torn between the instinct to abandon herself fully to the delights offered, and the desire to lessen her ultimate self-disgust. But even these emotional struggles were futile, for Craig was too strong for her. He meant to bend her to complete surrender, and she forgot all else save the moment, giving herself up gladly and generously to his kisses, gathering from life this one short interlude of bliss, when Craig was all her own. He took his lips from hers and her eyes sought his, a little fearful lest he should discover the secret within their depths. Her mouth was softly parted as if in readiness to be kissed again. A smothered little laugh escaped him, tinged with triumph – and with mockery.

'Is that the way Çetin kisses you?' he asked softly. 'And is that the way you respond? You're not so cold after all, I somehow didn't think you were.'

A terrible little silence followed. Jeanette felt he had struck her a blow and the colour drained from her face as she pushed her fists against his chest, releasing herself from his slackened hold. A tide of shame and humiliation swept over her both at the realization of the tumult within her and at the thought of her willing and eager surrender. How he must be despising her; and she deserved it, for she had known, all the time she was receiving those tender gentle kisses, that she was harming Diane. It was an odd philosophy in the world of men, she mused bitterly, that although their own lapses were excused, such lapses in women were condemned.

Craig's face above her, contemptuous and faintly mocking, aroused in her an irrepressible desire to hit back, to wipe that half sneer from his dark and arrogant face and she said, forcing a laugh,

'Poor Diane; she wouldn't like you to be kissing another girl.'

'Diane?' Craig cast her a swift glance. 'Diane won't find out,' he remarked, without expression. 'I shan't be fool enough to tell her, and I'm sure you will also remain silent about our . . . little indiscretion.'

Her colour rose at that and she bit her lip in vexation. She didn't quite know how her intended revenge had misfired, but it certainly had done so, in fact, it would appear that Craig had turned the tables on her, for she was the one feeling embarrassment while he stood there completely unperturbed by her reference to Diane.

She turned, with a trembling sigh, and took up her coat from the back of the chair. The little ball of terror in her throat had dissolved, but in its place had come that more familiar ache of loneliness and despair. She looked across at Craig, standing there, so tall, so coldly remote, and a blur of weariness darkened her vision.

'You're all in,' he observed, the inflection in his tones oddly at variance with the stern set lines of his jaw. 'I expect it's those kids – and your late night—' He broke off abruptly as she shot him an accusing, reproachful glance, and a flicker of amused comprehension touched the corners of his mouth. He hesitated a moment, and she felt sure he was considering some sardonic remark about what had just occurred, but all he said was, 'To-morrow is Saturday, so you can have a lie in.' He crossed the room, and had opened the door when she said, absently fingering one of the buttons on her coat,

'Neither the children nor the late nights will be affecting me soon; I expect Mark told you that I'm returning to England with him in December.'

He turned, slowly, an unfathomable expression on his face.

'No, Mark didn't mention it.' He took a step back into the room. 'This is a very sudden decision. You're breaking your contract?'

'My resignation has gone in. It's a mere formality, for I'm going home whether it's accepted or not.'

There followed a tense, uncomfortable silence, and a puzzling one too, for just as, a short while ago, Craig's anger had filled the car, so it now seemed to pervade the room. But no indication of anger sharpened his voice, on the contrary, he spoke in quiet tones, with that clipped, impersonal quality she knew so well.

'I think perhaps you've made a wise decision,' and turning again towards the door, 'Good night, Jeanette. Do as I say and have a rest in the morning.'

She saw him out, closed the door and leant against it, her fingers moving convulsively, pressing into the folds of her coat, her tears imprisoned in a black cloud of despair. At last she went upstairs and into her room. The curtains were apart; noiselessly she moved across the thick carpet to close them, shutting out the myriad lights on the strait, and on the distant shore, shutting out the dark silhouette of the trees surrounding Craig's house, and the graceful yacht outlined like some giant bird against a star-flecked amethyst sky.

CHAPTER ELEVEN

It was Sunday and Jeanette had slept at the flat, for Mark and Tony had gone to an all-night party along with Craig and Diane. Jeanette had also been invited, but as she had no wish to suffer more heartache, she had declined the invitation and asked her friends if she could spend the night with them. She was on the camp bed in the sitting-room and she lay there, comfortable and warm, for a long while after the first glimmer of dawn had wakened her. But as the objects in the room became more clearly defined she sensed a strangeness about the light and, rising, she slipped into a dressing-gown and went over to the glass door leading to the balcony.

A gasp of wonder left her lips as she stared, spell-bound, lost in a strange and mystic world of whiteness and of silence.

Snow had fallen steadily during the night, creating a dramatic, fairy-tale like scene, with the shining waters of the Bosphorus lending an air of charm and mystery possible only in the east. The domes of the mosques, glowing like giant pearls, were set in a bed of ivory; the minarets grew crystal stalagmites towards the sombre roof of the sky.

But even while she stood there, gazing in silent admiration, and with a totally new awareness of her surroundings, the clouds parted and a cascade of sunbeams escaped, drenching the scene with gold, painting the waters of Marmara with tints of ochre and spreading a pale brilliance over the mouths of the Bosphorus and the Golden Horn.

Turning as she heard the rattle of crockery in the kitchen, Jeanette went to join Sally who was making morning tea.

'I could have done that,' she apologized, reaching for

the tray. 'I've been awake ages. Have you looked outside?'

Sally nodded, reminding her that she and Gwen had already seen one Turkish winter.

'I'll never forget looking out for the first time, though, on a scene like this. You get used to it, but this first scene is the one that remains impressed for ever upon your mind.' The kettle began to boil and Sally made the tea while Jeanette put out the cups and saucers. 'It's a pity, in a way, that you won't see the real winter here.' Sally put the cosy over the teapot, eyeing her friend strangely. 'You never said what made you decide to go home.' She spoke tentatively, as if afraid of intruding on Jeanette's privacy, yet at the same time displaying a natural curiosity.

Jeanette found the sugar bowl and placed it on the tray.

'You didn't . . . guess?'

A small silence, and then,

'We thought it might be Craig Fleming,' she murmured, and Jeanette glanced away, a hint of colour rising. Sally added, in a gentle voice. 'You knew all the time about Diane, though?'

'Yes, Sally, I knew. I've been very foolish.'

'But he's not the sort for you,' her friend protested forcefully. 'Oh, I know he's devastatingly attractive, and he's obviously no pauper, but the man himself – I'll never forget the night of the party, the way he stood in that doorway, so darned superior, with that smouldering expression in his eyes. And you were nothing to him! Just imagine how you'd have felt if you'd been his wife. You'd have been terrified. I know I would, for the way he looked I'd have expected to be half killed when he got me home!'

Mechanically Jeanette put the spoons in the saucers, her thoughts flying to that night and a shudder passing through her at the memory. But had she been Craig's wife she wouldn't have been out without him, so she would have had nothing to fear.

'Shall I take a cup of tea in to Gwen?' she asked, changing the subject. 'Is she awake?'

'She wasn't when I got up. I'll go and see.'

Gwen was still sleeping and the two friends took their tea into the sitting-room.

'Were you comfortable?' inquired Sally, eyeing the bed. 'I see you didn't need the extra blanket.'

'No, I was lovely and warm.' She sipped her tea and was lost in thought. Only a few more days in Istanbul, for she and Mark had promised their parents they would be home for the new year. They should have been home for Christmas, but, much to Jeanette's astonishment, Mark had changed his plans. Craig was responsible for this, having persuaded her brother to accept an invitation to a party he was giving on Christmas Eve. Fortunately Jeanette had a legitimate excuse for not accepting his invitation, for she had already made arrangements to go out to a dance with her friends and the rest of the crowd.

'Have you seen much of Craig since that night?' Sally put milk in her cup and poured herself some more tea. 'I know Diane came over soon afterwards, but she went back, you said.'

'She came over to stay, at least, I imagine she intended staying, but her solicitor sent for her. She'd forgotten to sign some papers, so there were complications over her husband's estate. But she's here now – came over the day before yesterday, so Mark tells me. As for Craig, I haven't seen him for about a month.' She paused, a frown spreading. 'We're to dine with him tomorrow evening, and as there's to be only the four of us I can't very well get out of it, much as I would like to.'

She had thought up numerous excuses, since the invitation had come, but they were all so lame, and so obvious, that she had been reluctantly compelled to discard them all. But even when she was dressed and waiting for Mark to come from his room, fears began to assail her. It wasn't merely the prospect of spending a long evening watching Craig's tender display of affection for Diane which dismayed her, but she very much doubted her own ability to meet Diane without betraying her guilt. Craig she knew would be unruffled, confident, that his indiscretion, as he termed it, would remain for ever a secret. It appalled and disgusted Jeanette to think that a man could love as deeply and sincerely as he loved Diane and yet be willing to indulge in an affair with another woman – for assuredly an affair would have developed had he had his own way. It just went to prove that basically all men were alike, not averse to infidelity so long as they could escape discovery. She dwelt for a space on the picture she had built up of Craig; she had believed him to be fine and honourable, and while one part of her condemned his faithlessness, the other knew only pain at the thought of his being no better than any other man.

Her brother came downstairs and she faced him resolutely.

'I've changed my mind,' she told him quietly. 'I can't go with you to Craig's.'

'You—?' He stared at her incredulously. 'You're not coming?'

'It's impossible. I'm sorry, Mark. Apologize for me, please.'

'But you can't let Craig down, not at this late hour. It's not done. He'll have everything ready.'

'I'm sorry,' she said again. 'I'd rather stay at home.'

'But what on earth can I tell him? You can't do this, Jeanette.'

'Tell him I've a headache – or something.'

'That's a lame excuse,' he flashed, and her eyes filled up at his impatient tones. 'I'm not telling a lie like that! Besides,' he added, 'what am I going to feel like, sitting there while he and Diane make eyes at one another?'

Jeanette bit her lip. She hadn't thought of that. Nevertheless, her resolve did not weaken.

'It's no use. I just can't go.' Her distress seemed to register, for Mark's brow cleared a trifle.

'You've been avoiding him like the plague for the past few weeks. Is there something I don't know of? What's happened to make you like this?'

She cast him a startled glance and sought for a diversion.

'It's too intimate, with just the four of us. If there were other guests it wouldn't be so bad. But even Mrs. Fleming won't be there.'

'You knew there were no other guests invited – and that Craig's mother intended visiting this old friend of hers. Why did you accept the invitation?'

'I thought I'd be able to go through with it,' she replied unhappily, 'but I know I can't. Please try to understand, Mark.'

'I've no need to try to understand; I know how you feel. But this little dinner is put on specially for us, because we're going home. And you won't be there.' She said nothing, and after a little while he shrugged resignedly. 'I'll not be too late,' he said. 'But don't wait up for me – unless you want to, that is.'

She opened the door for him; a flurry of snow came in and sprinkled the carpet.

'You're not walking?'

'No, I'll take the car. Seems ridiculous for such a short distance, but there's no point in walking in this foul weather.'

She closed the door after him and went into the sitting-room. The only illumination came from the fire, where the pine logs glowed, throwing out an orange light to soften the shadows. Taking a magazine from the couch, Jeanette sat down on the rug, and began turning the pages, but her thoughts were with her brother. She felt guilty, and a coward, but she also felt there was an excuse for her conduct and hoped Mark would think up some convincing excuse for her non-appearance.

Craig would undoubtedly be annoyed, but that wasn't anything new. In any case, she wouldn't be affected by his annoyance. She began to wonder if he'd really wanted them to dine with him and Diane, and came to the conclusion that he had invited them merely because it was the polite thing to do, seeing that they were shortly to leave Istanbul for good.

Through the mist of her thoughts came the sound of a car, purring softly up the drive, and a slight frown crossed her brow. Why should Mark come back? It didn't sound like his car; odd how the snow softened the noise of the engine. Then she heard the bell. Mark wouldn't ring? And it wouldn't be Sally or Gwen, for they thought she was going out. She listened for Metat opening the door, was aware of his soft voice speaking in Turkish – and her eyes widened as she caught the abrupt, imperious tones of her visitor. Her heart began to thud unevenly as the door opened and she turned to see Craig standing there, his face a thunder cloud despite the softening effect of the snow on his eyebrows and hair. A smouldering glance told him that her decision was a last-minute one, for she still wore her cocktail dress.

'I invited you to dinner.' The door shut with an ominous little click and Craig leant against it, appearing even taller and broader than usual in his heavy tweed overcoat, with the storm collar turned up protectingly against his throat. 'Do you normally give back word five minutes before a meal is to be served?' In contrast to his expression his tones were low – but dangerously emphasized for all that. Her nerves fluttered and she stared across at him in bewilderment. Never for one moment had it occurred to her that he might react in this way.

'I— Didn't Mark tell you I had a headache?' She tried to rise, but her legs had lost the power of movement and she just sat there, absently pressing her fingers into the thick pile of the rug.

'He did,' Craig remarked drily, 'but Mark isn't a very good liar; I didn't believe him.'

She was all confusion.

'I'm sorry, but I didn't feel like going out. You shouldn't have left Diane – and Mark. Oh, dear, the dinner will be ruined,' she added, as the thought occurred to her.

'They'll get theirs.' Craig advanced slowly into the room, unbuttoning his coat as he did so. 'And I don't suppose either will notice whether the dinner is spoiled or not – the way they're feeling at present.'

'The way they're feeling?' she echoed blankly, again trying to rise. But she was too surprised to move, for Craig was taking off his coat, obviously preparing to stay. She watched, fascinated, as he folded it and laid it over the back of the couch. 'I don't know what you mean?'

'I left them sorting out their future.' He spoke curtly, moving towards the fire. 'They've discovered they're in love.'

'They've – they've—!' Jeanette gaped at him, unable to comprehend this staggering pronouncement. It wasn't possible! Only a short while ago Mark had expressed his reluctance to go alone to Craig's, because of the embarrassment of sitting there watching Craig and Diane 'making eyes at each other' as he had termed it. 'Mark and – and Diane?'

'I expect they're planning a spring wedding,' he returned calmly, coming closer.

Bereft of speech, she continued to stare at him. And yet even as she groped with the sudden chaos of her mind she recalled the several occasions when she had wondered about her brother's feelings for Diane. Diane's manner too had been puzzling at times, especially when they were on the island. She had almost flirted with Mark on one occasion. But despite these revealing flashes of memory, Jeanette could think only of the way Craig had waited all these years and she murmured, on an unconscious note of indignation,

'They can't be in love! It's quite impossible.'

Craig was right above her, his jaw set, an unfathomable expression in his eyes. Swiftly she averted her head, feeling somehow to blame for what her brother had done. He extended a hand to her.

'Get up,' he commanded.

Dazed by his action, she took his hand, quivering at the contact, and scrambled to her feet. He seemed to be waiting for her to speak.

'Craig ... if this is true—?' It must be true, she reluctantly concluded, for why else would Craig be here? Mark and Diane ... how could they do this to him? 'I'm so sorry,' she whispered huskily, looking up with wide, compassionate eyes. She could find no words with which to convey her sympathy, for she felt that whatever she said would cause him embarrassment. 'I can't imagine what's happened – in this short time – but I can understand why you had to come away. You couldn't stop there and see them – see them—' She broke off, flushing with dismay at her clumsiness. Craig must be feeling terrible, and she was only adding to his misery. 'I don't know what to say,' she ended lamely. They were standing very close; Jeanette made to free her hand with the intention of moving away, but it was retained in a firm and slightly hurtful grip.

'You've adequately expressed your pity for my broken heart—' His grip tightened as he spoke and she winced. 'Now,' he said with wrathful force, 'we'll change the subject. You can let me have the real reason for shirking my company this evening.'

'I wasn't shirking—' She stopped, almost intimidated by his darkening glance. There was something wrong; his attitude was certainly not that of the rejected lover. 'I just didn't feel like going out—'

'Don't lie! From the very beginning you've shirked the inevitable. I know you care for me – have done for some time – but you've persisted in fighting against it. Be honest and admit it!' She was too dumbfounded to utter a word and her silence gave the wrong impression, increasing his anger. 'Do you think you can go on evading me?' He gave her a little shake. 'Admit that you love me – I'll make you!' He held her away from him and she managed to stammer,

'Y-yes, I d-do love you, Craig,' feeling she would have said it, whether it were true or not, simply to pacify him, for he looked almost ready to murder her. 'But I wouldn't let you see because of—'

'I know full well why you wouldn't let me see! But this is the end, I've had enough!' She was drawn, almost brutally, into his embrace and a far from gentle kiss was forced upon her. 'I've been patient far too long. There's to be no more dwelling in the past. You're going to marry me – and like it!'

'M-marry you?' she managed to gasp, shaken by his rough handling. 'But you're in love with Diane.' The words didn't ring true, even to her own ears, and her heart began to race. But her mind was still in a state of chaos and the only picture it gave up was of Craig, hurt and embittered by the loss of Diane to his best friend, trying to find solace in marrying someone else. Her instinct was to express angry indignation at being chosen as the victim, but she prudently curbed it and began to point out, in what she hoped was a reasonable and sympathetic way, that while his reaction was perhaps a natural one, on being jilted after waiting all those years, she felt sure he would very soon come to regret having asked her to marry him. She was about to continue, to offer advice as best she could, but again her voice tailed off, for his eyes had darkened even more ominously. She felt his hands move from her waist, and she twisted round, away from the fire, and away from Craig. But he took her arms, jerking her back, and she steeled herself, sure he meant to shake her. However, if that were his original intention he changed his mind, and stood holding her, his lips compressed. A glimmer of memory brought back those occasions when his proprietorial attitude had been that of a man whose authority had some basis; he was now adopting a similar attitude – and Jeanette became enveloped in a sort of breathless expectancy.

'May I ask what makes you think I'm in love with Diane?' he inquired, with commendable control.

'Everybody knows—'

'Everybody?'

'Mark told me about what happened when you were both young, and how you had to part. And then your mother, she was very definite—' She stopped abruptly, realizing she had said too much. Craig's eyes glinted coldly, and he demanded to know what his mother had said about Diane and himself.

Jeanette couldn't tell him, and to her relief he seemed to understand and didn't press her, though his glance became oddly perceptive.

'So Mark told you that Diane and I were waiting to be married?' He did not give her the chance to reply, but added in a thoughtful tone, 'That rumour appears to have caused a good deal of trouble, one way and another.' His anger had left him and a faint smile appeared to relieve the stern set of his jaw. 'I'm not in love with Diane – haven't been for about fourteen years – so my asking you to marry me is not the natural reaction, as you term it of being jilted.' He paused and then, softly, 'I happen to love you, Jeanette.' His touch became gentle and his face relaxed and was softened by the curling flames as he half turned towards the fire. With infinite tenderness he took her into his arms and kissed her. She was breathless when at last he slackened his hold; her heart was acting most unnaturally and she could not speak for a while because of the emotion within her. She was no longer in doubt, yet it was so hard to believe that after a time she looked up, timidly, from under her lashes and said, as if in a dream,

'It can't be true. . . .' But she nestled close again, her head against his shoulder and a sigh of sweet contentment on her lips. 'Craig. . . .'

'My love?' His lips caressed the top of her head. 'What is it, darling?'

'Mark and Diane? Mark did think you and Diane would marry when her husband died.' Even as she spoke Jeanette recalled that her brother had once hinted –

though so vaguely that it had not registered with her at the time – that Diane and Craig might no longer be in love. Fifteen years was a long time, Mark had said, and people change.

'Diane and I did have a love affair. . . .' He tailed off smiling reminiscently for a moment. 'The sort of affair one has at nineteen – and for a while we both felt the world had come to an end when we were forced to part. But the very fact that we could part demonstrates the real strength of our – love. We've always remained friends, mainly I suppose because my mother has been a constant companion of Diane, and has helped her enormously during the past difficult years. I have a great admiration for Diane, but that isn't love, Jeanette.'

'But you've remained single all these years.' Somehow, that wasn't the right thing to say, and she added, to hide her slip, 'Mark thought it was because of Diane. He thought you and she were going to marry— He did, Craig, right up to about an hour ago. What happened?'

'Diane and I had been talking before dinner, and I asked her outright if she cared for Mark.' He glanced at her in some amusement and added, 'As for my remaining single all these years, I've been waiting for you, my sweet.'

She blushed adorably, and spoke in haste, ignoring his flattering comment.

'You asked her?' She leant away, blinking at him uncomprehendingly. 'You had an idea she might be in love with him?'

'It came to me in a flash when we were at the *yali*. It was the way she looked at him. How Mark missed it I don't know. I suppose it was because, as you've said, he was under the impression that she cared for me.' He drew her close again and kissed her lingeringly. 'That's what I meant just now when I said the rumour has caused a deal of trouble.'

'What did Diane say when you asked her?'

'She admitted that she cared for him,' he said, and

Jeanette was reminded of that coquettish glance which Diane had cast at Mark when they were all at the *yali*, examining the tapestry. That must have been the look to which Craig referred. 'And as I had suspected for some time that Mark was in love with Diane, I simply told him, as I let him in tonight, that he could go ahead and ask her to marry him.'

'You—' Jeanette stared. 'You said that?'

'I'd had enough complications with my own love affair,' was the grim rejoinder. 'I didn't see the sense of allowing theirs to become involved.'

'Wasn't Mark surprised? He thought he was going to play – that is. . . .'

'Play gooseberry?' Craig's brow lifted in amusement. 'Yes, I expect he did, with you not coming. He was more than surprised, mainly because Diane and I had, recently, been – er – rather affectionate towards each other.'

'Yes.' She glanced up swiftly, puzzlement in her eyes. 'Especially that night when Mark and I came to dinner. You – you were ever so loving to her.'

Craig paused for a moment as if reluctant to explain. But her anxiety touched him and he no longer hesitated.

'I'd told Diane of my feelings for you, and of your determination never to marry because of your dead fiancé—'

'It wasn't that – at least, it was at first, but soon I knew that Ned would never have wanted me to be unhappy and lonely all my life. No, Craig, that wasn't the reason I was determined not to marry.'

'I know that now, but I didn't then. Mark told me, before you arrived, about your tragedy, and that you were clinging to a memory. I wasn't interested – until I saw you. I knew almost immediately that you were the girl for me—'

'You couldn't have,' she interrupted swiftly. 'You ignored me for a month – often acted as if I weren't even there.'

'Only because of what Mark had told me. As soon as I realized how my feelings were I decided the most prudent course would be to leave you entirely alone.' He paused for a moment, shaking his head and smiling faintly. 'It was no use; I just had to make you love me. But I gradually became more and more frustrated at not being able to make any headway. As I said, Diane knew how I felt about you, and it was her idea to make you jealous. She said it was bound to work. She knew, being a woman, but somehow it misfired.'

Jeanette's lips quivered at the memory. She said, in tones barely above a whisper,

'Oh, Craig, it did hurt. On the verandah when you were waiting for Mark and me – you were holding hands. . . .' Her voice was not quite steady as she went on, 'You were so affectionate towards her – and to think you were only trying to make me jealous.'

'What a muddle! There was I, believing you were obstinately clinging to a memory, and you, darling, thinking I was to marry Diane. But surely,' he added in soft and gentle tones, 'you could tell that I cared. We were often so close, and I was so patient—'

A tremulous little laugh cut him short.

'Patient! How can you say that? – after threatening me the way you have! You've made me quite afraid of you.'

'Don't tell me any of your fibs. You're not in the least afraid of me!' His eyes narrowed, and he looked dark and rather formidable as the flames from the fire died down and the room became bathed in shadow.

'You did frighten me once,' she reminded him, and then wished she could take back her words; she wanted him to forget that party, and the way she was dressed.

'I'm making no excuses for that,' he returned inflexibly. 'I could have killed you – and Rustem! It's lucky for you that you weren't my wife! If I frightened you it's only what you deserved, although,' he added with a mingling of anger and indignation, 'I never intended the sort of mischief you seemed to be worried about. I wouldn't have expected you to think of me as that sort of blackguard.' She remained silent, burying her face in his coat as a flush of guilt spread at the recollection of her conclusions regarding his character. To her dismay Craig seemed anxious to see her expression, and he put a hand under her chin, tilting up her face. 'You did!'

'It was the way you kissed me,' she explained, penitently, and in some haste. 'And with your saying Mark was sleeping – it was the *way* you said it, Craig. You really did frighten me.' She nestled against him again and he felt the tiny shudder that passed through her. That sobered him and he said gently,

'But what about later, darling? You responded to my kisses then.'

She looked up, her eyes revealing all her love. Fleetingly she remembered that after he had achieved his desire, and forced the response from her, he had made that wounding reference to Çetin. But she understood now, with all the profound knowledge of a woman deeply loved, that anything he had done that night to hurt her had been born of jealousy.

'I couldn't help it, even though I thought I was cheating Diane.' Shyness overcame her suddenly as she added, 'I loved you so much, Craig.'

'I knew you did, but you'd just said there couldn't ever be anything between us, and I felt so utterly beaten.' His lips caressed her hair, and as they stood together in silence the room gradually became darker as the logs burned down to mere embers. 'Sweetheart,' he said at last, 'don't you think we'd better go and join the others?' He held her away, smiling in some amusement. 'I never thought I'd so forget my manners as to invite a friend to dinner and then walk out on him!'

Jeanette's smile broke in response; she did not question Craig about what had happened when Mark, turning up without her, tried to convince him she had a headache.

The smouldering glance Craig had given her on entering the room was explanation enough.

'Yes, I expect we ought to go. I'll get my coat.'

They came out into a white and silent world where everything glistened and soon they were travelling slowly along the Ortaköy Caddesi, on a blanket of snow. After a little silence Craig said in low and tender tones,

'My darling, you haven't said when you'll marry me?'

She hesitated, sensing his surprise as she did so.

'Craig ... your mother won't be pleased,' she had to say, thinking of the letter she had read at the *yali*, and at the same time hoping Craig would not insist on an explanation of her words.

'I understand my mother very well,' he said calmly, 'and I'm not going to pretend that she'll be pleased – quite the contrary in fact. But she'll accept you, and come to love you, I'm sure. In any case,' he added, still in the same calm voice, 'you won't have mother-in-law trouble, for we shan't be living in England.' He took her hand and placed it on his knee, asking again when she would marry him.

'My mother expects me home in a couple of days,' she began, when he interrupted her.

'You can write and tell her you're being married and the visit will be delayed.' His tones were firm, but he did go on to ask if her mother would be very disappointed at not having her home for the new year.

'She'll be so delighted with the news that she won't mind in the least.' Her mother would be glad for Mark, too, for she had long since despaired of his ever getting married. Jeanette hesitated, suddenly shy, and then, 'A double wedding would be nice, don't you think?'

'I do, but it so happens that Mark and Diane will have to wait a few months – for the sake of decency – while I, my child, am not willing to wait even a few weeks.' He fell silent, concentrating on his driving as he felt the wheels spinning beneath him. Skilfully he brought the car out of a skid, keeping his speed low as he prepared to turn off the Caddesi. Away in front the illuminations of the old city gleamed and twinkled like stars on a Christmas tree while in the distance the lights of a passing ship provided the only relief in the seemingly endless void of Marmara. Across the strait snow lay deep on the hills, like a glacier cascading down to the sea and on the Bosphorus itself the familiar lights flickered and multiplied themselves in the dim and turbulent waters. Turning into the drive, Craig gingerly touched the brake; the car slid to a standstill outside the brilliantly lighted front porch of the house. 'Can you be ready in a fortnight?' he asked, his arm around her shoulders.

Jeanette's eyes sparkled, but she replied demurely, and with a fluttering of her lashes,

'That's very short notice, but I'll try.'

'You'll try, eh?' His eyes were dark with amused perception but his voice was terse. 'That's very obliging of you, my dear, but I've been kept waiting quite long enough. You'll marry me in a fortnight, understand?'

'Yes, Craig,' she answered meekly, and lifted her face for his kiss.

Romance Treasury

An exciting opportunity to collect treasured works of romance! Almost 600 pages of exciting romance reading in each beautifully bound hardcover volume!

You may cancel your subscription whenever you wish! You don't have to buy any minimum number of volumes. Whenever you decide to stop your subscription just drop us a line and we'll cancel all further shipments.

FREE!

**A hardcover Romance Treasury volume
containing 3 treasured works of romance
by 3 outstanding Harlequin authors ...**

**... as your introduction to Harlequin's
Romance Treasury subscription plan!**

**... almost 600 pages of exciting romance reading
every month at the low cost of $6.97 a volume!**

A wonderful way to collect many of Harlequin's most beautiful love
stories, all originally published in the late '60s and early '70s.
Each value-packed volume, bound in a distinctive gold-embossed
leatherette case and wrapped in a colorfully illustrated dust jacket,
contains...
- 3 full-length novels by 3 world-famous authors of romance fiction
- a unique illustration for every novel
- the elegant touch of a delicate bound-in ribbon bookmark...
  and much, much more!

Romance Treasury

... for a library of romance you'll treasure forever!

Complete and mail today the FREE gift certificate and subscription
reservation on the following page.